I0692429

Patty's Fortune

BY

CAROLYN WELLS

Author of
The TWO LITTLE WOMEN *Series*
The MARJORIE *Books*
etc.

GROSSET & DUNLAP, *Publishers*
NEW YORK

PATTY'S FORTUNE

CONTENTS

CHAPTER I

AN INVITATION

"I THINK Labour Day is an awfully funny holiday," remarked Patty. "It doesn't seem to mean anything. It doesn't commemorate anybody's birth or death or heroism."

"It's like Bank Holiday in England," said her father. "Merely to give the poor, tired business man a rest."

"Well, you don't specially need one, Daddy; you've recreated a lot this summer; and it's done you good,—you're looking fine."

"Isn't he?" said Nan, smiling at the finely tanned face of her husband.

The Fairfields were down at "The Pebbles," their summer home at the seashore, and Patty, who had spent much of the season in New England, had come down for a fortnight with her parents. Labour Day was early this year and the warm September sun was more like that of midsummer.

[9]

The place was looking lovely, and Patty herself made a pretty picture, as she lounged in a big couch hammock on the wide veranda. She had on a white summer frock and a silk sweater of an exquisite shade of salmon pink. Her silk stockings were of the same shade, and her white pumps were immaculate.

Mr. Fairfield looked at the dainty feet, hanging over the edge of the hammock, and said, teasingly, "I've heard, Patty, that there are only two kinds of women: those who have small feet, and those who wear white shoes."

Patty surveyed the feet in question. "You can't start anything, Dad," she said; "as a matter of fact, there's only one kind of women today for they all wear white shoes. And my feets are small for my age. I wear fours and that's not much for a great, big girl like me."

"'Deed it isn't, Patty," said Nan; "your feet are very slender and pretty; and your white shoes are always white, which is not a universal condition, by any means."

"You're a great comfort, Nan," and Patty smiled at her stepmother. "Dunno what I'd do without you, when the Governor tries to take a rise out of me."

"Oh, I'll buy your flowers, little girl," and

Nan smiled back, for there was great friendship and chumminess between these two. "Are you tired, Pats? You look—well,—interestingly pale."

"Washed out, you mean," and Patty grinned. "No, I'm not exactly tired, but I've been thinking——"

"Oh, then of course you're exhausted! You oughtn't to think, Patty!"

"Huh! But listen here. This is Monday, and between now and Saturday night I've got to go to fourteen different functions, of more or less grandeur and gaiety. Fourteen! And not one can I escape without making the other thirteen mad at me!"

"But, Patty," said Mr. Fairfield, "that's ridiculous. Of course, you can refuse such invitations as you choose."

"Of course I can't, Lord Chesterfield. I've got to show up at every blessed one,—or not at any. I'd like to cut the whole caboodle!"

"Why don't you?" asked Nan. "Just retire into solitude, and I'll say you're suffering from—from——"

"Temporary mental aberration!" laughed Patty. "No, that wouldn't suit me at all. Why, this afternoon, I'm going to a Garden

[11]

Tea that I wouldn't miss for a farm. There's to be a new man there!"

"Well, just about the last thing you need on this earth is a new man!" declared her father. "You've a man for every day in the week now, with two thrown in for Sunday."

Patty looked demure. "I can't help it," she said. "I'm that entertaining, you know. But this new man is a corker!"

"My child, what langwich, what langwich!"

"'Tisn't mine. That the way he was described to me. So, of course, I want to see if he *is* any good. And, you won't believe it, but his name is Chick Channing!"

"What!"

"Yes, it is. Chickering Channing, for long, Chick for short."

"What *was* his mother thinking of?"

"Dunno. Prob'ly he was named for a rich uncle, and she couldn't help the combination."

"Who is he?"

"One of Mona's Western friends. Arrives today for a week or so. Mona's Tea is in his honour, though she was going to have it anyway."

"Well," said Mr. Fairfield, judicially, "of course you must go to that Tea, and subjugate

[12]

An Invitation

that young man. Then have him over here and I'll size him up. If you want him, I'll buy him for you."

"Thank you, dear Father, but I have toys enough. Well, then, tonight is the Country Club Ball. And I do hate that, for there are so many uninteresting people at it, and you have to dance with most of them. And tomorrow there's a poky old luncheon at Miss Gardiner's. I *don't* want to go to that. I wish I could elope!"

"Why don't you, Patty?" said Nan, sympathetically; "cut it all, and run up to Adele's, or some nice, quiet place."

"Adele's a quiet place! Not much! Even gayer than Spring Beach. And, anyway, it isn't eloping if you go alone. I want to elope with a Romeo, or something exciting like that. Well! for goodness gracious sakes' alive! Will you *kindly* look who's coming up the walk!"

They followed the direction of Patty's dancing blue eyes and saw a big man, very big and very smiling, walking up the gravel path, with a long, swinging stride.

"Little Billee!" Patty cried, jumping up and holding out both hands. "Wherever did you descend from?"

[13]

"Didn't descend; came up. Up from the South, at break of day,—Barnegat, to be exact. How do you do, Mrs. Fairfield? How are you, sir?"

Farnsworth's kindly, breezy manner, condoned his lack of conventional formality, and with an easy grace, he disposed his big bulk in a deep and roomy wicker porch chair.

"And how's the Giddy Butterfly?" he said, turning to Patty. "Still making two smiles grow where one was before? Still breaking hearts and binding them up again?"

"Yes," and she dimpled at him. "And I have a brand-new one to break this afternoon. Isn't that fine?"

"Fine for the fortunate owner of the heart, yes. Any man worthy of the name would rather have his heart broken by Patty Fairfield than—than—to die in a better land!"

"Hobson's choice," said Mr. Fairfield, drily. "Are you here for a time, Farnsworth? Glad to have you stay with us."

"Thank you, sir, but I'm on the wing. I expected to spend the holiday properly, fishing at Barnegat. But a hurry-up telegram calls me up to Maine, instanter. I just dropped off here over one train, to catch a glimpse of Little

Sunshine, and make sure she's behaving her-self."

" I'm a Angel," declared Patty, with a heaven-ward gaze. "And, Bill, what do you think! I was just saying I wanted to elope. Now, here you are! Why don't I elope with you?"

" If it must be some one, it might as well be me," returned Farnsworth, gravely; " have you a rope ladder handy?"

" Always keep one on hand," returned Patty, gaily. "When do we start?"

" Right away, now, if you're going with me," and Bill laughed as Patty sat up straight and tied her sweater sash and pretended to get ready to go.

" But this is the strange part," he went on; " you all think I'm fooling, but I'm not! I do want to carry Patty off with me, on this very next train."

" This is so sudden!" said Patty, still taking it as a joke.

" You keep still a minute, Milady, and let me explain to your elders and betters." Patty pouted at this, but Bill went on. "You see, Mr. Fairfield, I'm involved in some big busi-ness transactions, which, not to go into details, have made it necessary for me to become the owner of a large hotel up in Maine,—in the lake region."

" I thought all Maine was lakey," put in Patty.

" Well, this is a smallish lake, not far from Poland Spring. And it's a big hotel, and it's to close tomorrow, and all the guests will leave then. And I've got to go up there and look after it."

" How did you happen to acquire this white elephant?" asked Fred Fairfield, greatly interested.

" Had to take it for a debt. Man couldn't pay,—lost his money in war stocks.—I'll tell you all about it while Patty's getting her bag packed."

" What do you mean?" cried Nan, seeing Farnsworth's apparent sincerity.

" Oh, Lord, I forgot I haven't told you yet! Well, as I have to go up there for a week or two, and as the hotel is all in running order, and as all the guests are going off in a hurry, and the servants are still there, I thought it would be fun to have a sort of a house party up there—"

" Gorgeous!" cried Patty, clapping her hands, " Who's going, Bill?"

" That's the rub! I haven't asked anybody

[16]

yet, and I doubt if I can get many at this time of year."

"Haven't asked anybody! I thought you had planned this house party!"

"Well, you see, I just got the telegram last night, and it was on the train coming up here this morning that I planned it—so the plans aren't—aren't entirely completed as yet."

"Oh, you fraud! You made it all up on the spur of the moment——"

"Yes'm, I did. But what a spur the moment is! Now, see here, it's clear sailing. We can get the Kenerleys and they'll be the chaperons. Now, all we have to do, is to corral a few guests. You and I are two. How about Mona Galbraith?"

"She'd go if she could," said Patty, "but she's having a party this afternoon. Chick Channing is over there."

"Chick Channing! Is he really? Well! Well! I haven't seen that boy for years. We must make them come. And Daisy? Is she there?"

"Yet, but don't get too many girls——"

"Don't be alarmed, you little man-eater, you! The Farringtons will go, maybe; and Kit Cameron and his pretty cousin. Oh, I've a list of possibles, and we'll get enough for a jolly little

[17]

crowd. You've no objections, have you?" and Farnsworth looked anxiously at the elder Fairfields.

"N-no," began Nan, "but it isn't all clear to me yet. Suppose the Kenerleys can't go?"

"That puts the whole plant out of commission. Unless,—oh, by Jove! wouldn't you two go? That would be fine!"

But Mr. Fairfield and Nan refused to be drawn into any such crazy scheme. It was all right for young people, they said, but not for a comfort-loving, middle-aged pair.

"Well, I'll tell you," said Farnsworth, after a moment's thought. "I'll get the Kens on the long distance, and find out for sure. Meantime, Butterfly, you be packing a few feathers, for sumpum tells me Adele will go, anyway, whether old Jim does or not."

"Might as well throw some things in a suitcase I s'pose," said Patty; "it's better to be ready and not go than to go and not be ready."

After a long session at the telephone, Bill announced a triumphant success. The Kenerleys would be glad to go. Moreover, Adele would meet Patty and Bill in New York that very day in time for a late luncheon. Then they would get the Farringtons and the others by telephone. Then Patty would go home with Adele for the night, and they would all go to Maine the next day.

"You see it's very simple," said Bill, with such an ingenuous smile that Nan went over to his side at once.

"Of course it is," she agreed. "It's simply lovely! And Patty wanted to get away from the giddy whirl down here. She'll have the time of her life!"

But Mr. Fairfield was not so sure. "I think it's a wild goose chase," he said. "What sort of a place are you going to? You don't know! What sort of service and creature comforts? You don't know! What will you get to eat? You don't know! That's a nice sort of outlook, I must say!"

"Oh, easy now, sir. It isn't as bad as all that. I've had rather definite and detailed reports, and if it weren't all comfy and certain, I wouldn't take Patty up there. It's a Lark, you see, a Lark,—and I'm sure we'll get a lot of fun out of it. And, incidentally, I know it's a fine section of country,—healthful, invigourating, and all that. And the house is a modern up-to-date hotel. They always close soon after Labour Day, but this year, owing to circumstances, it's the very day after. That's where the fun comes in, having a whole hotel all to ourselves. But we must be getting on. The train leaves in twenty minutes."

"I'm all ready," said Patty, as she re-appeared, miraculously transformed into a lady garbed for travelling. A silk pongee coat protected her gown and a small hat and veil completed a smart costume.

"I don't altogether like it——" began Mr. Fairfield, as they got into the motor to go to the train.

"Run along, Patty," said Nan. "I'll see to it that he does like it, before you leave the station. Going to Mona's?"

"Yes, just for a minute. You see her as soon as we're gone, and tell her all about it. We can only say the barest facts."

They flew off, Patty's veil streaming behind, until she drew it in and tied it round her neck.

At Red Chimneys, several young people were playing tennis, but Patty called Mona to her and told her briefly of the plan.

"Glorious!" cried Mona. "If it were not for that old Tea, we could go right along now. But we'll come tomorrow. Where shall we meet you?"

An Invitation

Quickly Farnsworth told her, and then turned to see his old friend, Channing.

"Chick, old boy!" he cried. "My, but it's good to see you again!"

Channing was presented to Patty, who looked at him in amazement. He was the biggest man she had ever seen, even taller than Bill Farnsworth. He looked enormously strong, and when he smiled, his large mouth parted to show two rows of big, white, even teeth, that somehow made Patty feel like Red Ridinghood before the wolf. But there was little time for getting acquainted, for it was almost train time.

A few words between the two men as to meeting next day, and then the motor flew to the station.

And only just in time, for though Bill handed Patty on to the steps with care, he had to scramble up himself as the train was about to start.

"How do you like eloping?" he said, smilingly, as they rolled away.

"Fine," said Patty, dimpling, "but must it always be done in quite such a hurry?"

"Not always; next time we'll take it easier. Now, let's make a list of our house guests."

Farnsworth took out a notebook and pencil, and they suggested various names, some

[21]

of which they decided for and some against.

At last Patty said, in an assured tone, "And Phil Van Reypen."

"Not on your life!" exclaimed Bill. "If he goes *I* don't!"

"Why, Little Billee, we couldn't have the party at all without *you!*"

"Then you'll have it without *him!* See?"

Patty pouted. "I don't see why. He's an awfully nice man, I think."

"Oh, you do, do you? Why don't you stay home, then, and have him down at the sea-shore to visit you?"

"Oh, that wouldn't be half as much fun. But up there is that lovely place, all woodsy and lakey and sunsetty, I could have a splendid time, if I had all my friends around me." Patty's sweet face looked very wistful, and Farnsworth scanned it closely.

"Does it mean so much as that to you, Patty? If it does, you shall have him invited."

"Oh, I don't care. It's your party, do just as you like."

"Because it's my party, I want to do just as *you* like." Bill spoke very kindly, and Patty rewarded him with a flash of her blue eyes, and the subject was dropped.

CHAPTER II

THE HOTEL

"THIS is a little like a real eloping, isn't it?" and Bill gave Patty's suitcase to a porter, whom they followed across the big Pennsylvania station in New York.

"A *very* little," said Patty, shaking her head. "You see it lacks the thrill of a real out-and-out elopement, because people know about it. An elopement, to be any good, must be a secret. If ever I get married, I'm going to elope, that's one thing certain!"

"Why, Patty, how unlike you! I thought you'd want a flubdub wedding with forty-'leven bridesmaids and all the rest of it."

"Oh, I s'pect I shall when the time comes. I often change my mind, you know."

"You bet you do! You change it oftener than you make it up!"

"Why, I couldn't——" began Patty, and just then they reached the taxicab rank, and Bill put Patty into a car.

[23]

They went to the Waldorf, where they were to meet the Kenerleys, and found that Jim and Adele had just arrived.

"What a perfect scheme!" exclaimed Adele, as soon as greetings had been exchanged. "Who all are going?"

"Let us go to luncheon," said Bill, "and then we can thrash out things. I reserved a table— ah, here we are," as the head waiter recognised the big Westerner.

"I love to go round with Bill," said Patty, "he always has everything ready, and no fuss about it."

"He sure does," said Jim Kenerley, in hearty appreciation. "But the way he scoots across the country and back, every other day or two, keeps him in trim. He lives on the jump."

"I do," agreed Farnsworth. "But some day I hope to arrange matters so I can stay in the same place twice running."

Laughing at this sally, they took their places at the table, which Bill's foresight had caused to be decorated with a low mound of white asters and maidenhair fern.

"How pretty!" cried Patty. "I hate a tall decoration,—this is just right to talk over. Now, let's talk."

The Hotel

And talk they did.

" I just flew off," Patty declared, as she told Adele about it. " Nan's going to pack a trunk and send it, when she knows we're truly there. I think she feared the plan would fizzle out."

" Indeed it won't," Bill assured them. " We've got the nucleus of our party here, and if we can't get any more, we can go it alone."

But it was by no means difficult to get the others. Some few whom they asked were out of town, but they responded to long distance calls, and most of them accepted the unusual invitation.

Farnsworth had a table telephone brought, and as fast as they could ring them up, they asked their guests.

The two Farringtons were glad to go; Marie Homer and Kit Cameron jumped at the chance. Mona and Daisy, with Chick Channing, would come up from the shore the next day, and that made eleven.

" Van Reypen? " asked Kenerley, as they sought for some one to fill out the dozen.

" Up to Patty," said Bill, glancing at her.

" No," and Patty shook her golden head, slowly; " no, don't let's ask Phil this time."

"Why not?" said Adele in astonishment. "I thought you liked him."

"I do; Phil's a dear. But I just don't want him on this picnic. Besides, he's probably out of town. And likely he wouldn't care to go."

"Reasons enough," said Farnsworth, briefly. "Cross off Van Reypen. Now, who for our last man?"

"Peyton," said Jim. "Bob Peyton would love to go, and he's a good all-'round chap. How's that, Bill?"

"All right, Patty?" and Bill looked inquiringly at her.

"Yes, indeed. Mr. Peyton's a jolly man. Do you think he'd go, Adele?"

"Like a shot!" Kenerley replied, for his wife. "Bob's rather gone on Patty, if you know what I mean."

"Who *isn't* gone on Patty?" returned Farnsworth. "Well, that's a round dozen. Enough!"

"Plenty," Patty decreed. And then the talk turned to matters of trains and meetings and luggage.

"I'll arrange everything for the picnic," said Bill. "You girls see about your clothes and that's all you need bother about. You'll want

The Hotel

warmish togs, it gets cool up there after sundown. Remember it's Maine!"

Patty and Adele at once began to discuss what to take, and Patty made a list to send to Nan for immediate shipment.

"What an enormous piece of humanity that Chicky is!" said Patty, suddenly remembering the stranger. "Do you know him, Jim?"

"Yes; known him for years. He's true blue, every inch of him. Don't you like him, Patty?"

"Can't say yet. I only saw him half a jiffy. But, yes, I'm sure I shall like him. Bill says he's salt of the earth."

"He's all of that. And maybe a little pepper, as well. But you and old Chick will be chums, I promise you. Now we'll pack you two girls off to Fern Falls, and I'll do a few man's size errands, and Bill, here, will make his will and dispose of his estate, before going off into the wilderness with a horde of wild Indians. Then tomorrow, he'll pick us up at Fern Falls, and we'll all go on our way rejoicing."

"Not so fast," said Adele, after Jim finished his speech. "You two men can go where you like, Patty and I will take a taxi, and do some last fond lingering bits of shopping, before we

[27]

go home. Don't you s'pose we want some shoes
and veils and——"

"Sealing-wax?" asked Farnsworth, laughing.
"All right, you ladies go and buy your milli-
nery, and I'll see you again tomorrow on the
train."

As might have been expected, with such capable management, everything went on smoothly,
and it was a clear, bright afternoon when they
completed the last stage of their journey, and
the train from Portland set them down at their
destination.

Not quite at their destination, however, for
motorbuses were in waiting to take them to the
hotel itself.

For more than an hour they bumped or glided
over the varying roads, now through woods,
and now through clearing.

At last, a vista suddenly opened before them,
and they saw a most picturesque lake, its dark
waters touched here and there by the setting
sun. It was bordered by towering pines and
spruces, and purple hills rose in the distance.

"Stunning!" cried Patty, standing up in the
car to see better. "I never saw such a theatrical lake. It's like grand opera! Or like the

castled crag of Drachenfels, whatever that is."

"I used to recite that at school," observed Chick Channing; "so it must be all right, whatever it is."

And then, as they turned a corner, the hotel itself appeared in sight. An enormous structure, not far from the lake, and set in a mass of brilliant salvias and other autumn flowers and surrounded by well-kept velvety greensward.

"What a peach of a hotel!" and Patty's eyes danced with enthusiasm and admiration. "All for us, Little Billee?"

"All for we! Room enough?"

"I should say so! I'm going to have a suite, —maybe two suites."

"Everybody can have all the rooms he wants, and then some. I believe there are about five hundred——"

"What?" cried Daisy Dow, "five hundred! I shall have a dozen at least. What fun!"

The cars rolled up to the main entrance. Doormen, porters, and hallboys appeared, and the laughing crowd trooped merrily up the steps.

"I never had such a lark!" declared Mona. "Oh, I've seen hotels as big,—even bigger,— but never had one all to myself, so to speak. Isn't it just like Big Bill to get up this picnic!"

Marie Homer looked a little scared. The vastness of the place seemed to awe her.

"Chr'up, Marie," laughed her cousin, Kit Cameron. "You don't have to use any more rooms than you want. How shall we pick our quarters, Farnsworth?"

"Well, let me see. Mr. and Mrs. Kenerley must select their rooms first. Then the ladies of the party; and, if there are any rooms left after that, we fellows will bunk in 'em."

So, followed by the whole laughing troop, Adele and Jim chose their apartments. They selected two elaborate suites on the second floor, for Bill told them that there were scores of servants, and they were better off if they had work to do.

"Isn't it heavenly?" sighed Elise Farrington, dropping for a moment on a cushioned window-seat, in Adele's sitting-room, and gazing at the beautiful view. "I want my rooms on this side of the house, too."

"All the girls on this side," decreed Adele, "and all the men on the other. Or, if the men want a lake view, they can go up on the next floor. If I have to comfort you girls, when you're weeping with homesickness, I want you near by. Marie, you're most addicted to nostalgia, I recommend you take this suite next to mine."

So Marie was installed in a lovely apartment, next Adele's and with practically the same view of the lake and hills.

Daisy's came next, then Mona's, and Patty's last. This brought Patty at the other end of the long house, and just suited her. "For," she said, "there's a balcony to this suite, and if I feel romantic, I can come out here and bay the moon."

"You'll do nothing of the sort, young woman," said Adele, severely. "You do that moon-baying act, and you'll be kidnapped again."

"No, thank you," and Patty shuddered, "I've had quite enough of that!"

The rooms were beautifully furnished, in good taste and harmonious colourings. The hotel had been planned on an elaborate scale, but for some reason, probably connected with the management, had not been successful in this, its first season; and in swinging a business deal of some big lumber tracts in that vicinity, it had fallen into Farnsworth's hands. He had no inten-

[31]

tion of keeping it, but intended to sell it to advantage. But at present, it was his own property and he had conceived the whim of this large-sized picnic.

"Boom! Boom!" sounded Channing's deep bass voice in the hall. "That's the dressing-gong, people. Dinner in half an hour. No full dress tonight. Just a fresh blouse and a flower in your hair, girls."

"Isn't he great?" said Patty to Mona, as they responded through their closed doors.

But the girls' suites of rooms could all be made to communicate, and they ran back and forth without using the main hall.

"He is," agreed Mona, who was brushing her hair at Patty's dressing-table. "And the more you see of him, the better you'll like him. He's shy at first."

"Shy! That great, big thing shy?"

"Yes; he tries to conceal it, but he is. Not with men, you know,—but afraid of girls. Don't tease him, Patty."

"Me tease him!" and Patty looked like an injured saint. "I'm going to be a Fairy Godmother to him. I'll take care of him and shield him from you hoydens, with your wiles. Now, go to your own rooms, Mona. I should think,

[32]

with half a dozen perfectly good rooms of your own, you might let me have mine."

"I can't bear to leave you, Patty. You're not much to look at,—I know,—but somehow I forget your plainness, when——"

Mona dodged a powder-puff that Patty threw at her, and ran away to her own rooms.

Half an hour later, Patty went slowly down the grand staircase.

Adele had decreed no evening dress that first night, so Patty wore a little afternoon frock of flowered Dresden silk. It was simply made, with a full skirt and many little flounces, and yellowed lace ruffles fell away from her pretty throat and soft dimpled arms. Its pale colouring and crisp frilliness suited well her dainty type, and she looked a picture as she stood for a moment halfway down the stairs.

"Well, if you aren't a sight for gods and little fishes!" exclaimed a deep voice, and Patty saw Chickering Channing gazing at her from the hall below. "Come on down,—let me eat you."

As Patty reached the last step, he grasped her lightly with his two hands and swung her to the floor beside him.

"Well!" exclaimed Patty, decidedly taken

[33]

aback at this performance. "Will you wait a minute while I revise my estimate of you?"

"For better or worse?"

"That sounds like something—I can't think what—Declaration of Independence, I guess."

"Wrong! It's from the Declaration of Dependence. But why revise?"

"Oh, I've ticketed you all wrong! Mona said you were shy! *Shy!*"

"Methinks the roguish Mona was guying you! Shyness is *not* my strong point. But, if you prefer it should be, I'll cultivate it till I can shy with the best of them. Would you like me better shy?"

"Indeed I should, if only to save me the trouble of that revision."

"Shy it is, then." Whereupon Mr. Channing began to fidget and stand on one foot, then the other, and even managed to blush, as he stammered out, "I s-say, Miss F-Fairfield,——"

It was such a perfect, yet not overdone burlesque of an embarrassed youth, that Patty broke into peals of laughter.

"Don't!" she cried. "Be yourself, whatever it is. I can't revise back and forth every two minutes! I say, Mr. Chickering Channing, you're going to be great fun, aren't you?"

"Bid me to live and I will live, your Funny-man to be. Whatever you desire, I'm it. So you see, I am a nice, handy man to have in the house."

"Indeed you are. I foresee we shall be friends. But what can I call you? That whole title, as I just used it, is too long,—even for this big house."

"You know what the rest call me."

Patty pouted a little. "I never call people what other people call them."

"Oh, Lord, more trouble!" and Chick rolled his eyes as if in despair. "Well, choose a name for yourself——"

"No, I want one for you!"

"Oh, what a *funny* young miss! Well, choose, but don't be all night about it. And I warn you if I don't like it, I won't let you use it."

"'*Shy!*' Oh, my!" murmured Patty. "Well, I shall call you Chickadee, whether you like it or not."

"Oh, I like it,—I *love* it! But, nearly as many people call me that as Chick!"

"And I thought it was original with me! All

[35]

right, I'll think up another, and I shan't speak to you again until I've thought of it."

Nonchalantly turning aside, Patty walked across the great hall to where a few of the others had already gathered.

"Pretty Patty," said Kit Cameron, in his wheedling way; "wilt thou stroll with me, after dinner, through the moonlight?"

"She wilt not," answered Adele, for her. "Look here, young folks, if I'm to chaperon you, I'm going to be pretty strict about it. No strollings in moonlights for yours! If you want gaiety, you may have a dance in the ballroom. The strolling can wait till tomorrow, and then we'll all go for a nice walk round the lake."

"A dance!" cried Patty, "better yet! Who would go mooning if there's a dance on? I'll give you the first one, Kit. Oh, you haven't asked for it, have you?"

"But *I* have, Patty," said Farnsworth's voice over her shoulder, "will you give it to me?"

"I promised Kit," said Patty, shortly, and then she turned to speak to Bob Peyton about a golf game next day.

CHAPTER III

A MIDNIGHT MESSAGE

DINNER in the big dining-room was great fun. A large, round table had been prepared for the party, and the smaller, unoccupied tables all about, were also decorated with flowers to give a festive atmosphere.

As there were scores of idle waiters, each of the party could have one, or more, if desired.

Farnsworth seated his guests.

"I'll sit here," he announced, "and I'll ask Mrs. Kenerley to sit at my right. The rest of you may sit where you choose, alternating, of course, the girls and the men. Now, here's my plan. At every meal, the men sit as we do tonight, and the ladies move one seat to the right. This gives us new companions each time, and prevents monotony."

"Here's me," said Patty, dropping into the chair at Bill's left hand, while Channing sat the other side of Patty. Laughingly, they all found places, and dinner was served.

[37]

It was an unusual experience. The hotel dining-room was ornate in design and appointments, and its green and gold colouring and soft glow of silk-shaded lights made a charming setting for the merry party round the big table. The other tables, and there were many of them, looked as if they might be occupied by the ghosts of the departed guests.

"It's like being castaways on a beautiful and very comfortable desert island," said Patty, as she looked appreciatively at a huge tray of hors d'œuvre offered her by a smiling waiter. "I do love these pickly-wickly things, and never before have I felt that I might take my time in choosing. But, here at——what's the name of the hotel, Bill?"

"Never mind the name on its letter-heads," he returned, "we'll call it Freedom Castle. Everybody is to follow his or her own sweet will,—or somebody else's if that seems pleasanter."

"Who has the pleasantest will?" asked Patty, looking around; "I want to follow it."

"I have," said Chick, promptly. "My will is something fierce in the way of pleasantness. I daresay every one here will fall all over them-

[38]

selves in their haste to follow it. Ha, do I hear a familiar strain? I do!"

He did, for just then the hotel orchestra, a fine one, struck up a popular air.

"Music, too!" exclaimed Mona. "All the comforts of home, and none of the cares. This is just too perfect! Billy Boy, you're a wonder!"

"To think of it being Bill's hotel!" said Daisy, in an awed voice.

"To think of our being here without any bills," put in Roger Farrington. "That's the best part of it. It's like being given the freedom of the city!"

"The freedom of the country," Adele corrected; "that's much better."

The orchestra, on a platform, gorgeous in scarlet, gold-braided coats, began a fascinating fox-trot.

Kit Cameron looked across the table at Patty, with a nod of invitation.

Smiling assent, Patty rose, flinging her napkin on the table. Kit came round to her, and in a moment they were dancing to the music that had called them. Skilfully, Kit guided her among the maze of tables and chairs, for they were the two best dancers in the crowd, and they had no difficulty in avoiding obstacles.

"Have a turn, Adele?" asked Bill, laying down his fork.

"No, thank you; it's all very well for the girls, but your chaperon is too nearly middle-aged for such capers."

"Nonsense; but maybe you're wise to save your energies for an evening dance."

Several of the young people did dance a few turns, but Chick Channing speedily caused them to halt by announcing the arrival of mushrooms under glass.

"Whoosh!" cried Kit, "back to nature! We can dance at any old time, but mushrooms under glass are an event! I say, Bill, I'm glad the cook didn't leave with the guests."

"The whole serving force is under contract for a fortnight longer," explained Farnsworth. "You can live on mushrooms, if you like."

"It's Paradise," said Marie Homer, ecstatically; "I don't ever want to go home. Does the mail come regularly?"

Everybody laughed at Marie's look of anxiety, and Bill replied, "Yes, my child, you can get your daily letter from him up here."

"He doesn't write *every* day," said Marie, so innocently that they all roared again.

"I wish *I* had somebody to write love-letters to me," sighed Patty. "It must make life very interesting."

"I'll write them to you," offered Chick. "It's no trouble at all, and I'm the little old complete love-letter writer."

"You're right here in the spot, though, so that's no fun. I mean somebody who isn't here,—like Marie's somebody."

"Well, you must have plenty of absent adorers. Can't you encourage their correspondence?"

"But then I'd have to write first, and I hate to do that, it's so—so sort of forward."

"That, to be sure. But it's better to be forward than forlorn."

"Oh, I'm not exactly forlorn!" said Patty, indignantly. "I can be happy with all these others, if t'other dear charmer *is* away."

"Can you, Patty?" whispered Bill. "Are you happy here?"

"Oho, Little Billee, I am beatifically happy! Just see that confection Louis is bringing in! Could I be anything but happy with that ahead of me?"

The dessert that had just appeared was indeed a triumph of the confectioner's art. Composed of ice cream, meringue and spun sugar, it was built into an airy structure that delighted the sight as well as the palate. Everybody applauded, and Adele declared it was really a shame to demolish it.

"It would be a shame not to," said Patty, her blue eyes dancing in anticipation of the delicious sweet.

"What a little gourmande you are," said Chick, watching Patty help herself bountifully to the dessert.

"'Deed I am. I love sweet things, they always make me feel at peace with the world. I eat them mostly for their mental and moral effect on me, for my disposition is not naturally sweet, and so I do all I can to improve it."

"And yet you give the effect of a sweet dispositioned person."

"She is," spoke up Daisy, overhearing. "Why, Chick, Patty is the sweetest nature ever was. Don't you believe her taradiddles."

"I know the lady so slightly, I'm not much of a judge. But I feel sure she'll improve on acquaintance," and Chick looked hopeful.

A Midnight Message

"I hope so, I'm sure," and Patty's humble expression of face was belied by the twinkle in her eye.

Then dinner was over, and Adele rose and led the way to the great salon or drawing-room.

"Come for a little walk on the veranda," said Chick to Patty. "Let's get more acquainted."

Patty caught up a rose-coloured wrap from the hall rack, and they went out and strolled the length of the long veranda that went round three sides of the house.

"Splendid crowd," said Chick, enthusiastically; "and right down fine of old Bill to do this thing."

"He *is* fine," said Patty, impulsively; "whatever he does is on a big scale."

"His friendships are, I have reason to know that. He's done heaps for me, dear old chap."

"Have you known him long?"

"Three or four years. Met him through Mona. Good sort, Mona."

"Yes, Mona's a dear. She's the sort that wears well. Where is your home, Mr. Chick?"

"Nowhere, at present. I've lived in Arizona, but I've come East to grow down with the

[43]

country. I'm a mining engineer, at your service."

"I'd love to employ you, but, do you know, I seldom have need of the services of a first-class mining engineer."

"Oh, I'm not so awfully first-class. Bill thinks he can use me in his manœuvres. We talked it over a bit on the way up, and I hope so, I'm sure."

"Then I hope so, too."

"Thank you. You're a kind lady. Shall we sit in this glassy nook and flirt a bit?"

They had reached a portion of the veranda, glass-enclosed, and arranged with seats among tall palms and jars of flowers. There were shaded lights and a little illuminated fountain in the centre.

"I'll stop here a moment, but I can't flirt," said Patty, demurely; "my chaperon won't allow it."

"Allowed flirting is no fun, anyway. Forbidden fruit is sweetest."

"But sour grapes are forbidden fruit. How can sour be sweet?"

"Oh, it's all according to your nature. If you have a sour nature, the grapes are sour. If a sweet disposition, then all fruits are sweet."

A Midnight Message

"Even a lemon?"

"Nobody hands a lemon to sweet people."

"Then they can't have any lemonade, and I love it! I guess I'll stop being so sweet——"

"Good gracious, Patty, you couldn't do *that* if you tried!"

This remark was made by Kit Cameron, who just then put his head in at the doorway and overheard Patty's laughing decision.

"Hello, you two," he went on; "you'll have to stop your introspective conversation, and come and join the dance. Will you, won't you come and join the dance? We're only to have one, our dragon chaperon declares, and then we must all go by-by. So come and trip it, Patty of the fairy toes!"

The trio returned to the drawing-room, and after the one dance had been extended to half a dozen, Adele collected her headstrong charges and carried them off to bed.

"And you're not to have kimono confabs all night, either," she ordered. "Patty, you'll be good for nothing tomorrow, if you don't get some rest. And the others, too."

But there was more or less chattering and giggling before the girls separated for the night. It seemed natural for them to drift into

[45]

Patty's boudoir and in their pretty negligées they dawdled about while Patty brushed her hair.

"What goldilocks!" exclaimed Marie, in admiration. And truly, Patty's hair was a thing to admire. Thick and curling, it hung well below her waist, and shone with a golden glimmer as the light touched its rippling lengths.

"It's an awful nuisance," Patty declared; "there's such a lot of it, and it does snarl so."

"Let me help you," cried Daisy, springing up and taking the brush from Patty's hand. "Mona, do the other side."

Mona seized another brush and obeyed, and as the two brushed most vigorously, Patty's little head was well pulled about.

"Thank you, girls, oh, *thank* you *ever* so much, but truly, I *don't* mind doing it myself! Oh, *honestly*, I don't!"

Patty rescued her brushes, and soon had the rebellious locks in two long pigtails for the night.

"Now, scoot, all of you," she said, "this is the time I seek repose for my weary limbs, on beds of asphodel—or—whatever I mean."

"Beds of nothing," said Mona, "I'm not a

[46]

A Midnight Message

bit sleepy. Let us stay a little longer, Patty, dear,—sweet Patty, ah, *do* now."

"*I* can't," and Marie started toward the door. "I'm awfully sleepy."

"You don't fool me, my infant," said Patty, wisely. "Your eyes are like stars burned in a blanket! *I* know what you're going to do! But don't be alarmed, I won't tell."

Marie blushed and with murmured good-nights, ran away.

"Going to write a letter, of course." And Daisy wagged her sapient head. "Who is the man, Pat?"

"Fie, Daisy! You heard me say I wouldn't tell!"

"You only said you wouldn't tell what she's going to do. And we know that. Do tell us who he is!"

"I won't do it. If Marie chooses, she will tell you herself. And anyway, Daisy, it's no one you know. I don't think you ever saw him and I doubt if you ever even heard of him."

"Is he nice?"

"Charming. Full of capers, though. And Marie is so serious. But he's very attractive."

"Are they engaged? Oh, Patty, *do* tell us about it!"

"I can't. I don't know so very much about it myself; but what I do know is a sacred trust, and not to be divulged to a horde of rattle-pates. Now, will you make yourselves scarce? Go and write letters, go and darn stockings,—anything, but let me go to bed."

Finally, Patty shooed the girls away, and locking her door against their possible return, she began to make ready for bed.

She glanced at her watch as she sat at her toilette-table. It was exactly midnight.

And at that moment her telephone rang.

"Those girls!" she thought to herself. "I'll not answer it!"

But the bell kept ringing, and Patty took down the receiver with a soft "Hello."

"That you, Patty?" and her astonished ears recognised Philip Van Reypen's voice.

"For mercy's sake! Where are you, Phil?"

"Home. In New York. Can you hear me all right?"

"Yes, plainly. How did you know I was here?"

"Learned it from your father. Say, girlie, why didn't you get me a bid up there, too?"

"Do you want to come?"

"*Do* I! Aren't *you* there!"

[48]

" Is that a reason? "

" The best in the world. Do get Farnsworth to invite me."

" I can't, Phil. He doesn't want any—any more than we have here now."

" You mean he doesn't want *me*."

" Why, doesn't he like you? " Patty's voice was full of innocent surpise.

" It isn't that, but he wants you all to himself."

" Nonsense! There are a dozen of us up here."

" Well, I mean he's afraid to have *me* there. By Jove, Patty, that's a sort of a compliment. He's afraid of me."

" Don't be silly, Philip. How's Lady Van? "

" She's all right. She's at Newport, just now. I'm in town for a day or two, so thought I'd call up Spring Beach and maybe run down there to see you. And this is the immediate result. Well, look here, Patty, if I can't get invited to Farnsworth's Palace Hotel, for I hear it's that, I'm going to Poland Spring, and then I can run over and see you anyway."

" Oh, Philip, *don't* do that! "

" Why not? Haven't I a right to go to Poland Spring, if I like? "

[49]

"Yes, but don't come over here."

"Why not?"

"I can't exactly explain it, myself; at least not over the telephone, but I don't think it would be nice for you to come here when you were not invited."

"Oh, I was spoken of, then?"

"Well,—yes,—since you will have it."

"And Farnsworth wouldn't have me?"

"Well,—I said not to have you."

"Oh, you *did!* What a nice friend you are!"

"Now, Phil, don't talk like that. I said— I said——"

"Bless your heart, I know just how it was. Or nearly. But you could have had me asked— and you didn't! Now, my lady, just for that, I *am* going to Poland Spring—start tomorrow. And,—listen, now,—if you really don't want me to come over to the Farnsworth House, then you must come over to the Poland Spring House to see me! Get that?"

"Why, Phil, absurd! How could I go alone?"

"You needn't come alone. Bring a chaperon, or another girl or a crowd of people if you like, or even a servant, but *come!* That's all, so good-night, little girl. Pleasant dreams!"

A Midnight Message

The telephone clicked as Phil hung up, and with a little gasp, Patty hung up her receiver and threw herself on a couch to think it over. She couldn't help laughing at the coil she was in, for she well knew she couldn't go to Poland Spring House, unless with the whole crowd,— or nearly all of them. She pictured Bill reaching there to be greeted by Philip Van Reypen! Dear old Bill; after all he had done to make it pleasant for them, to hurt his feelings or to annoy him in any way, would be mean. She wished Phil had kept out of it. She wished there wasn't any Phil nor any Little Billee, nor —nor—anybody,—and somehow Patty's long, brown lashes drooped over her pansy blue eyes, —and, still robed in her chiffon and lace peignoir, and all curled up on the soft, spacious couch,—she fell sound asleep.

CHAPTER IV

BLUE ROCK LAKE

IN a blaze of September glory, the sun shone across the lake. The leaves had not yet begun to turn, and the summer trees were as green as the stalwart evergreens, but of varying shades. From deep, almost black, shadowy forests, the range ran to brilliant, light green foliage, in a gamut of colour. Some of the younger and more daring trees crept down to the water's edge, but much of the lake shore was rocky and more or less steep. Here and there a picturesque inlet had a bit of sandy coast, but the main effect was rugged and wild.

But even the intrusive sun could only peep into Patty's boudoir through a chink or two between the drawn shades and the window frames. And so his light was not enough to wake the sleeper, still cuddled among the couch pillows.

But she was awakened by a bombardment of raps on the door.

[52]

"Patty!" called Daisy's impatient voice; "whatever *are* you doing? Open this door!"

The blue eyes flew open. But Patty was the sort of person who never wakes all at once. Nan always said Patty woke on the instalment plan. Slowly, and rubbing her eyes, she rose and unlocked the door.

"Why, Patty Fairfield!" Daisy exclaimed, "your lights are still burning! You—why, *look* at you! You didn't undress at all! You have on your evening petticoat and slippers! and the very same boudoir robe I left you in last night. And"—Daisy looked in at the bedroom door,—"your bed hasn't been slept in! What *is* the matter?"

Daisy rattled on so, that Patty, still half asleep, was bewildered. "I don't know——" she began, "Philip called——"

"Philip called! Patty, are you crazy? Wake up!" Daisy shook her a little and under this compulsion Patty finished waking up.

"Good gracious!" she exclaimed, laughing, "did I sleep there all night? No wonder I feel like a boiled owl."

"But why,—*why* did you do it?"

"Fiddlesticks, I don't know. It's no crime, I suppose. I lay down there for a few minutes,

[53]

Patty's Fortune

after you hoodlums cleared out, and I suppose I fell asleep and forgot to wake up. That's all. Lemme alone, and a bath and a cup of hot chocolate will restore my senses."

"You dear little goose! I'll run your tub for you. Though I suppose there are a string of maids waiting outside your door. Want 'em?"

"No, rather have you. But send half a dozen of them for some choclit, please."

Still yawning, Patty began to take off her slippers and stockings. "Thank you, Daisykins," she said, as Daisy returned from the bathroom. "Now, you light out, and I'll make a respectable toilette. My, how I did sleep. I was worn out. But I feel fine now. Good-bye, Daisy."

But Daisy was slow to take the hint.

"I say, Patsy, what did you mean by saying Philip called?"

Patty hesitated for the fraction of a second, and then decided it were wiser to keep her own counsel regarding that matter.

"Dreaming, I s'pose. Certainly, there was no Philip here in reality."

"But you said distinctly that Philip called," Daisy persisted.

"Well, s'pose I did? What could it have

been but a dream? Do you imagine I had a real, live caller?"

" No; but it must have been a vivid dream! "

" It was," said Patty. " Now scoot! "

Daisy scooted, and Patty locked her door again.

" Well, you're a pretty one! " she said to herself; " the idea of sleeping all night without going to bed. Adele will be terribly exercised over it. But I have other things to worry about. I wonder if Philip will really come up here, and if he does, what Bill will do. Would I better tell Bill about it? Or, just let the situation develop itself? Oh, what troubles some poor little Pattys do have! Come in! "

This last in response to a gentle tap at the hall door.

A trim maid entered with a tray.

" Oh, joy! " cried Patty; " I'm simply starving,——Mary, is it? "

" Sarah, ma'am," returned the girl, gazing admiringly at pretty Patty, who was now in a kimono of light blue silk, edged with swansdown.

" Well, Sarah, stay a few moments, and you can help me dress. Sit down there."

Sarah obediently took the small chair Patty

designated, and folded her hands on her immaculate frilled apron.

"Tell me about the hotel, Sarah," said Patty, as she crunched the crisp toast between her white teeth, and smiled at the maid.

"What about it, ma'am?"

"Well, let me see; how did you maids feel when you found the guests were leaving?"

"At first we feared we'd lose our money, miss; then we were told that our contracts held till the end of this month, and if we would stay as long as we were asked to, we'd get paid in full."

"Wasn't that nice?"

"Fine, ma'am. I'm using mine for my little sister's schooling, and I'd sore miss it."

"So all the servants were willing to stay?"

"Oh, yes, ma'am. You see, none could get good places up here. The hotels all have their own, and many of them will close the first of October."

"I see. Isn't it funny to have a dozen guests, and the rest of this big place empty?"

"It is, indeed, miss. Shall I get you some hotter chocolate?"

"No, I've finished, thank you. Now, you call somebody else to take the tray, and you stay to help me. I've taken a fancy to you, Sarah, and I want you for my personal maid while I'm here. Is that all right?"

"Yes, indeed, miss. I'm proud to do for you. But I'm not a trained lady's maid."

"Never mind, I'll train you."

Patty had a nice way with servants. She was always kind, and treated them as human beings, yet never was she so familiar that they presumed on her kindness. She soon discovered that Sarah, though untrained, was deft and quick to learn, and she instructed the maid in the duties required.

And so, when Adele came tapping at the door, she found Patty seated before the mirror, while Sarah was coiling the golden hair according to directions.

"Well, girlie, what's this I hear about your sleeping on a couch, when a perfectly good bed was all turned down for you?"

"Oh, just one of my whimsies," returned Patty, airily. Don't bother about it, Adele."

And Adele was wise and kind enough not to bother.

Soon, arrayed in a most becoming white serge, with emerald green velvet collar and cuffs and a pale green silk blouse, Patty descended the great staircase to find most of the party grouped there, about to start for a ramble round the lake.

" 'Course I'll go," she said in answer to eager inquiries. " My hat and gloves, Sarah, please."

" Yes, Miss Patty," and the maid, who had been following her, returned upstairs.

" I've adopted Sarah as my personal body-guard," Patty said. " You don't mind, Bill, do you ? "

" Not a bit ! " he replied heartily. " The house is yours and the fulness thereof. I hope all of you ladies who want maids, or keepers of any sort, will call on the service force for them."

Sarah came down then, bringing Patty's hat, a soft felt, green, and turned up on one side with a Robin Hood feather. It was most becoming, as Patty tilted it sideways on her head, adjusting it before a large mantel mirror.

" Now we're off," she said, gaily; " but we ought to have Alpenstocks, or swagger-sticks."

" Here are some," said Bill, opening a cupboard door, and disclosing a lot of long sticks. Everybody selected one, and they set forth.

" Such a wonder-place ! " exclaimed Marie, as at every fresh turn they found some new bit of scenery or different view. " I could stay here forever!"

" Me too!" agreed Mona. "What's the name of the lake?"

"Something like Skoodoowabskooskis," said Bill, laughing; "but for short, everybody calls it Blue Rock Lake."

" Because the rocks on the other side look so blue, I suppose," suggested Daisy.

" I believe you're right!" cried Chick, in mock amazement at her quick perception. Whereupon Daisy made a face at him.

"Don't mind him, Daisy," said Patty; adding, teasingly, "it's perfectly true, the distant rocks do look blue, hence the term, Blue Rock Lake,—blue rocks and the lake, see?"

"Oh, you smarty!" and Daisy lost her temper a little, for she hated to be made fun of; "if you tease me, I'll tease you. What about a girl who wakes up, babbling of some ' Philip ' or other!"

"Babbling nothing!" cried Patty. "And anyway, I'm always babbling, asleep or awake. Oh, see that bird! What a beauty!" As a matter of fact there was no bird in sight, but canny Patty knew it would divert attention from

Daisy's remark, and it did. After vainly looking for the beautiful bird, other distractions arose, and Patty breathed more freely that nobody had noticed Daisy's fling.

But after they had walked all round the lake, and were nearing the hotel again, Bill stepped to Patty's side and falling in step with her, put his strong, firm hand under her elbow, saying: "Want some help, little girl, over the hard places?"

Channing, who had been at her other side, took the hint and fell behind with some of the others.

"What's this about your waking up with Philip's name on your lips?" he said; "do you want to see him so badly? If so, I'll ask him up here?"

Patty hesitated; here was her chance to get the invitation that Phil so coveted, and yet, she knew Bill Farnsworth didn't want him. Nor was she sure that she wanted him, herself, if he and Little Billee weren't going to be friendly. A nice time she would have, if the two men were cool or curt to each other.

So she said, "No, I don't want him, especially. I daresay I was dreaming of him. I dream a lot anyway, of everything and everybody."

"Dreaming?" said Farnsworth, in a curious voice; "is that all, Patty?"

"All? What do you mean?"

"Is that all the communication you had with Van Reypen last night? In dreams?"

Patty looked up, startled. Did Bill know of the telephone message? Would he care? Patty felt a certain sense of guilt, though, as she told herself, she had done nothing wrong. Moreover, the only reason she had for not telling Farnsworth frankly of Phil's message, was merely to spare him annoyance. She knew he would be annoyed to learn that Phil had called her at midnight on the long distance, and if he didn't already know it, she would rather he shouldn't. But did he, or not?

"Pray, how else could I talk to him?" she said, laughingly. "Do you suppose I am a medium and had spirit rappings?"

"I suppose nothing. And I know only what you choose to tell me."

"Which is nothing, also. Why, Little Billee, you're in a mood this morning, aren't you?"

She glanced up into the face of the man who strode beside her. It was a fine face. Strong, well-cut features made it interesting rather than handsome. It was also a determined face, and full of earnestness of purpose. But in the blue eyes usually lurked a glint of humour. For the moment, however, this was not noticeable, and Farnsworth's lips were closed rather tightly,— a sure sign with him, of seriousness.

"Since you choose to tell me nothing, I accept your decision. But once more I ask you, for the last time, do you wish me to invite Van Reypen up here?"

A moment Patty thought. Then she said, "No, thank you, Billee, I don't."

Farnsworth's brow cleared, and with a sunny smile down at her, he said: "Then the incident is closed. Forget it."

"All right," and Patty smiled back, well pleased that she had decided as she did.

"You little goose!" said he, "I know perfectly well that you called up Van Reypen on the telephone last night."

"I did not!" declared Patty, indignantly.

"Now, Apple Blossom, don't tell naughty stories. I say, I *know* you did."

"All right, Mr. Farnsworth, if you doubt my word, there's nothing more to be said."

Patty was thoroughly angry, and when she was angry she looked about as fierce as a wrathy kitten. But, also, when Patty was angry, a few

[62]

foolish tears *would* crowd themselves into her eyes, and this only served to make her madder yet. She turned from him, wanting to leave him and join some of the others, but she couldn't, with those silly drops trembling on her eyelashes.

"Look up, Apple Blossom," said a gentle voice in her ear. Farnsworth's voice was one of his chief charms, and when he modulated it to a caressing tone, it would cajole the birds off the trees.

Patty looked up, and something in her blue eyes glistened through the tears, that somehow made her look incapable of "telling a naughty story."

"Forgive me, Posy-Face," Farnsworth murmured, "I *will* believe you, whatever you tell me. I will believe you, whether I think you're telling the truth or not!"

At this rather ambiguous statement, Patty looked a little blank. But before she could ask further explanation, they had reached the hotel and they all went in.

CHAPTER V

M'LLE FARINI!

ACCORDING to Farnsworth's plan, at luncheon, each girl moved her seat one place to the left. This put Adele at the host's left, and moved Patty on farther, so that she was between Jim Kenerley and Chick Channing.

"Welcome, little stranger," said Chick, as they sat down. "I'll have you now, and again tonight at dinner, sitting by me side, and then life will be a dreary blank, while you slowly jog all round the table, getting back to me, two days after tomorrow. How the time will drag!"

"You're so flattering!" and Patty pretended to be terribly pleased. But, as a matter of fact, she was wishing she could sit next Little Billee, and find out whether he was really angry at her. Also, she decided she would tell him all about the telephone message, for he apparently believed she had told him a falsehood. And, too, it occurred to her, that he might not make

[64]

any great distinction between calling and being called on the telephone.

"What do you think about it? Shall us go?" said Chick, and Patty realised, with a start, that she had been so lost in her thoughts, that she hadn't heard the talk at table.

"Go where?" she asked, looking blank.

"Oh, come back from dreamland, and learn what's going on. Cameron knows of a wonderful hermit, who lives in a shack in the woods and tells fortunes. Do you want to snatch the veil from the hidden future, and learn your fate?"

"Yes, indeed; I just love fortune tellers! Where is he, Kit?"

"Off in the woods, in a tumble-down old shanty. But he's the real thing in seers! I was out for an early morning prowl, and I discovered him. Bobbink, that's my pet bellhop, says he's greatly patronised by the populace, but though he gets lots of coin, he won't move into better quarters or disport himself more as a man of means."

"Well, I want to go to see him," Patty declared. "Will you go, Billee?"

"Can't go this afternoon, Patty; I'm sorry, but I have another engagement."

[65]

"So have I," said Daisy, looking a little conscious. "Let's leave Mr. Fortune Teller till tomorrow morning."

All agreed to this, and after luncheon was over, they proceeded to plan various sports.

"Tennis, Patty?" asked Chick.

"No; too poky." And Patty gave a restless gesture, most unusual with her, and only indulged in when she was bothered about some trifle. She wanted to get a moment alone with Farnsworth and tell him about Phil. She knew from the way Little Billee looked at her, or, rather, didn't look at her, that he was hurt or offended, or both.

"Golf then?" Chick went on.

"No, too slow."

"Well, how 'bout lawn bowls?"

"What are they?"

"Never tried lawn bowls! Oh, they're lots of fun. Come on."

In a short time they had collected half a dozen people and were in the midst of a gay game, when Farnsworth suddenly appeared, riding a big, black horse. Very stunning he looked, for his riding togs were most becoming and he sat his horse with all the grace and easy carelessness of the Western rider.

" Oh, Billee," cried Patty, dropping the bowling ball she was about to roll, " I want to go riding ! "

And then she was covered with chagrin, for Daisy came out of the hotel, also garbed in the trimmest of riding costumes, and a groom led a horse for her to mount.

" Do you, Patty ? " said Bill, not unkindly, but with a disinterested air. " You may. There are lots of horses in the stables."

Patty quickly recovered her poise. " Thank you," she cried, gaily; " a little later, then. Will you go, Chick? "

" Will I ! Just try me ! "

" Well, we'll finish this game, and then there will be time enough."

The game over, they went for a ride. Patty's riding habit was dark green, of modish cut and style. She was a good horsewoman, though she seldom rode. Channing, likewise, was a good rider, but he made no such picturesque effect in the saddle as Big Bill.

" Whither away? " he said, as they started.

" Is it too far to go over to Poland Spring House? "

" Not a bit. It's a goodish distance, but the road is splendid, and it isn't four yet."

So they set off briskly for that destination. The exhilarating air and exercise quite restored Patty's good humour, and she cast off all thought of petty botherations and enjoyed herself thoroughly.

"Great!" she exclaimed, smiling at Chick, as they flew along.

"Yes, isn't it? And it's not so very far, we're nearing the approach to the place now. We'll have time for tea, and get back well before dark."

"Lovely! Oh, what a big hotel! And *will* you look at the squirrels!"

Sure enough, the lawn and verandas were dotted with fat gray squirrels. They were very tame and had no fear of people or horses. They welcomed Patty and Chick, by sitting up and blinking at them as they dismounted and grooms took their horses away.

Asking for the tea room, they were shown the way, and ushered to a pleasant table.

"Chocolate for me, please," said Patty, as the waiter stood with poised pencil. "I hate tea. So chocolate, and dear little fussy cakes."

"Chocolate is mine, too, then. Whatsoever thou eatest that will I eat also. Well, by Jove, will you look over there!"

Patty looked in the direction that Chick's eyes indicated, and there, at a small table, busily eating cakes and tea, sat Farnsworth and Daisy Dow.

"Shall we join them?" asked Chick.

"Join them! Oh, no, they don't want joiners. They're absorbed in each other."

They did look so. Bill was earnestly talking and Daisy was listening with equal intentness. Her face was bright and animated, while Farnsworth's was serious and thoughtful.

Patty was angry at herself for being one whit disturbed at sight of them, thus chummily having their tea, and she tossed it off with a gay laugh. "Besides, I'd rather chat with you alone than to have a foursome."

"Good girl, Patty," and Chick nodded approvingly. "Do you know I think you're about as nice as anybody, after all."

"So do I you," and Patty sipped her chocolate with an air of contentment. "This is a much bigger hotel than ours, isn't it?"

"Yes, but ours is more beautiful, I think, and quite big enough for our party."

"Of course. Oh, what a stunning-looking woman! See, Chick, over toward your left."

Channing turned slightly to see a very hand-some dark-eyed woman, who smiled at him as their glances met.

"Why, bless my soul!" he exclaimed; "if it isn't Maudie Kent. I say, Patty, don't you want to meet her? She's an actress, or was, and she's a dear. Awfully good form and all that, and really worth while."

"Yes, I'd love to know her," said Patty, look-ing with interest at the stunning gown the lady wore. It was of flame-coloured silk, veiled with black net, and was matched by a wide hat of black with flame-coloured plumes.

"Excuse me a moment, then," and Channing rose and went over to where the lady stood. She was alone, and he had no difficulty in per-suading her to come to their table.

"You dear child," said Miss Kent, as Chan-ning introduced them; "how pretty you are! I'm so glad to know you. But what are you doing here with Chick Channing?"

"Just having tea," said Patty, smiling back into the big dark eyes that looked at her so kindly.

"But are you staying here? Where are your people?"

"We are staying over at Freedom Hall,"

she began, and then paused, for with those eyes upon her, she couldn't quite make it seem a rational thing to do.

" Oh, it's quite all right, Maudie," Channing put in, " there's a crowd of us, with chaperons and things, and our good host, by the way, is right across the room, at a tea-table."

" That good-looking chap with the pretty girl? Oh, it's Mr. Farnsworth! Mayn't I know her, too? "

" Now, see here, Maudie, you can't know everybody that I do. Be content with Miss Fairfield, at least for the present."

" Oh, I am, more than content. No, I'll have coffee, please. Chocolate is only for the very slim."

" Surely you are that," ventured Patty, glancing at the graceful form of the new acquaintance.

" But I wouldn't be, if I indulged in sweet things. Enjoy them while you may, my dear, in after years you'll be glad you did."

" What are you doing here, Maudie? " asked Channing. " Are you alone? "

" Yes; I'm having a concert tonight, and I'm in such trouble. You see," she turned to Patty, " I'm a sort of professional entertainer. I give concerts or recitals, and I get performers of the very best and usually they are most dependable and reliable. But tonight I have a concert scheduled, and my prima donna is lacking. If she doesn't come on this next train, I don't know what I shall do. I suppose I shall have to give back the ticket money, and call the affair off, and that means a great loss to me. For I have to pay the other performers their price just the same."

"That's a shame," said Channing, sympathetically. "But she'll surely come."

"I'm afraid not. I've telegraphed and I can't get her anywhere. I can't help thinking she deliberately threw me down because she received a better offer, or something of the sort. But I mustn't bore you with my troubles. Forget it, Miss Fairfield, and don't look so concerned."

"I'm so sorry for you," said Patty, "to go to all that trouble and expense, and have it all for nothing."

"Less than nothing," said Chick, "for you stand to lose considerable, I suppose."

"Yes, well over five hundred dollars. Oh, here are the motorbuses from the train. Now we'll see."

But though many guests arrived at the hotel the singer was not amongst them.

"No," said Miss Kent, scanning them sadly, "she isn't here. Oh, what shall I do?"

Patty's mind was working fast. She knit her brows as she tried to think calmly of a wild project that had come into her mind.

"Miss Kent," she began, and stopped; "I wonder—that is——"

"Well, my dear, what is it? Do you want to ask something of me? Don't hesitate, I'm not very terrifying, am I, Chick?"

"No, indeed. What is it, Patty?"

"Oh, of course, it wouldn't do,—I hate to suggest it, even,—but you see, Miss Kent, I can sing——"

"And Patty can impersonate the absent singer! And nobody would ever know the difference! Great!" cried Channing. "Oh, Maudie, your trouble is at an end!"

"Now wait," said Patty, blushing. "I am not a professional singer, but I have studied with good masters, and I have a voice, not so very big, but true. Forgive this plain speaking, but if I could help you out, Miss Kent, I should be so glad."

"You're a little darling!" exclaimed Maud

Kent; "I wonder if we *could* carry off such a thing. You see, your coming here, as you just did, a stranger, and talking to me only, looks quite as if you were the arriving singer. That part's all right. As to your voice, I have no doubts about that, for you *didn't* say you sang 'a little.' And any way, even a fair singer would do, in addition to the talent I have. But Miss Fairfield, I can't accept this from you. Will you take just the price I expected to give M'lle Farini?"

"I couldn't accept money, Miss Kent. That would be impossible. I'm glad to do this to help you out, for it's no trouble for me to sing, I love to do it. And don't bother about the payment. Give it to some charity, if you like."

"Oh, I can't accept your services without pay! But if you knew what a temptation it is!"

"Yield to it, then," and Patty smiled at the troubled face. "But first, you must hear my voice. You can't decide before that. Where can we go?"

"Come up to my apartment, no one will hear us there, and if they should, it's no great harm. One may practise, I suppose. You may come too, Chick, if you like."

The three left the tea-room, and as they disappeared through the door, Farnsworth caught sight of Patty's face.

"What does that mean?" he cried, so angrily that Daisy was startled.

"What does what mean?"

"Did you see who went out that door?"

"No; who?"

"Patty and Chick Channing and Maudie Kent."

"I know the first two, but who is Maudie Kent?"

"An actress! A woman Channing and I knew in San Francisco a good while ago. What can she be doing here? And how did she get hold of Patty? Though of course, Chick is responsible for that. But what are they up to? I'm going after them."

"Bill, don't do anything so foolish! Patty has a right to visit the lady if she wants to. It isn't your business."

"But Patty—with that woman!"

"Why, isn't she a nice woman?"

"She's an actress, I tell you."

"Well, lots of actresses are lovely ladies. Isn't this one?"

"Yes, of course, she's a lovely lady. But Patty oughtn't to be racing round with her."

"Patty wasn't racing! She wouldn't do such a thing in Poland Spring House. Now, Bill, put it out of your mind. There's no occasion for you to get stirred up because Patty has made a new acquaintance. And I guess Chick Channing can take care of her, he wouldn't let her know anybody who wasn't all right."

"Chick is thoughtless. He likes Maudie, and so do I. But she's no fit companion for Patty."

"Why? Is Patty Fairfield better than us common people? Is she made of finer clay? Wouldn't you want *me* to meet the Maudie lady?"

"Oh, you. Why, that wouldn't matter so much."

"Bill Farnsworth! What a speech! I guess I'm every bit as good as Patty Fairfield."

"Of course you are, Daisy. Don't be silly. But you're more—more experienced, you know, and a little less—less conventional. Patty has never had half the experience of the world that you have. I don't want her mixed up with that sort of people, and I won't have it!"

"Well," and Daisy spoke coldly, "I don't see how you can help it. They've gone off, and you can't very well follow them, or have them arrested. Probably Chick and Patty are start-

[76]

ing for home. And I'm sure it's time we did."

"But I can't go off and leave Patty here!"

"You can't do anything else. You're not Patty's keeper, Bill, and it's silly to act as if you were."

"That's so, Daisy." Farnsworth's fine face looked anxious and his eyes were sad. "Come on, I suppose we had better be going. I'll order the horses round."

Farnsworth kept a sharp eye out, but he saw no more of the trio who had left the tea room, and who had so disturbed him. In quiet mood he rode off at Daisy's side, and they went back to the hotel.

CHAPTER VI

MAUDE'S CONFIDENCES

MEANTIME, Patty, in Miss Kent's parlor, was singing her best. The scheme appealed to her very strongly. She was glad to assist the kind and beautiful lady, and moreover, she enjoyed an escapade of any sort, and this surely was one.

Miss Kent was delighted with her voice, and predicted an ovation for her. They selected several of Patty's best songs, and had the accompanist in to rehearse with her.

"What about dress?" said Patty, after it was positively settled that she was to sing at the concert.

"I'll ride over and get you whatever you want," said Channing, anxious to be of service.

"Oh, no," said Miss Kent, "that would be a shame for you to go to all that trouble. I have a little white tulle gown that can be made just right in a jiffy. I am a bit taller than Miss

Maude's Confidences

Fairfield, but a tuck will fix that. Now, here's an important point. You see, the notices and the programmes all say M'lle Farini will sing. Shall we let it go at that? I mean, let Miss Fairfield impersonate M'lle Farini, or shall we have an announcement made at the opening of the concert, that Miss Fairfield is acting as substitute?"

"I'd rather let it go without the use of my name," said Patty. "I don't know as it would be quite right, but I'd love to let people think I was the Farini lady. It would be such fun."

"Well," said Miss Kent, "let's just leave it. If we don't say anything of course the audience will take it for granted that you are M'lle Farini. And if any objections are raised, or if it comes out afterward, I can say that I had to substitute you at the last moment, and there was no time to have new programmes printed."

"That will be fine," Patty declared; "I do love a joke, and this is really a good one, I think. Yes, let me be M'lle Farini, for one night only, and if the real owner of that name objects, why, it will be all over then, and she'll have to take it out in objecting. But I shan't disgrace her, even if I don't sing as well as she does."

"But you do, Miss Fairfield," exclaimed Miss Kent; "she has a fuller, stronger voice, but yours has more melody and sweetness. You will remain here over night, of course."

"Oh, I never thought about that!" and Patty looked a little alarmed. "I don't know what Adele will say."

"Oh, please do. You really must. I have two bedrooms in my suite, and I can make you very comfortable."

"Well," and Patty hesitated; "I'll have to talk this thing over with Mrs. Kenerley. I'll telephone her now, and if she is willing, I will stay here all night."

So Patty called up Adele and told her the whole story.

Adele listened, and then she laughed, good-naturedly, and told Patty she could do as she liked. "I think it's a harum-scarum performance," she said, "but Jim says, go ahead, if you want to. You stay with your new friend all night. Of course you couldn't come home after the concert. I suppose Mr. Channing will stay at that hotel, too. And then he can bring you home in the morning. What will you wear?"

Patty told her, and then she asked Adele not to tell the others what she was up to. "I'm afraid they'll come over," she said; " and I can carry it through all right before strangers, but if all you people sat up in front of me, giggling, I couldn't keep my face straight, I know; so don't tell them till after it's over."

"All right, girlie, I will keep your fateful secret locked in my heart till you bid me speak. Have a good time, and sing your sweetest."

"Now that's all right," and Patty looked enchanted at the prospect of fun ahead. "I'm going to have the time of my life! You go away now, Chick, and Miss Kent and I will see about my frock. Shall we meet at dinner?"

"Yes, I want you two girls to dine with me. Do you know anybody, Maudie, to make a fourth?"

"No, wait, Chick. I don't want to dine in public. Nor do I want Miss Fairfield to be bothered with a company dinner. I'll tell you a better plan. She and I will dine alone, here in my little parlour. You get your dinner downstairs, by yourself, and then, after the concert is over, you can invite us to supper and we can talk it over."

Channing acquiesced, and then he went away, not to see them again until supper time.

"You are so good, Miss Fairfield——"

"Oh, do call me Patty. I like it so much better."

"I'll be glad to. And you must call me Maude. It is a perfect Godsend, your helping me out like this. May I tell you just a little bit about myself?"

"I wish you would. And I'm so glad I can be of service to you."

But first they must needs attend to the all-important matter of Patty's frock, and sure enough, a white tulle of Maude's was easily and quickly altered till it just fitted Patty. It was new and modish, made with full skirts and tiers of narrow frills. There was no lace or other trimming, save the soft tulle ruffles, and Maude decreed no jewelry of any sort, merely a few yellow roses at the belt,—the tiny mignon roses. These she ordered from the office, and by that time their dinner was served.

As they sat enjoying the few but well-chosen dishes that Maude had selected, she told Patty somewhat of her life, and Patty listened with interest.

"I have to support myself, my mother and a crippled sister," Maude said, "and I had ambition to become a great actress. But after a fair trial, I found I could be at best only a mediocre actress. I found, however, that I had talent for organizing and arranging entertainments, and I concluded I could make more money that way than on the stage. So I took it up as a regular business, and I have succeeded. But this year has not been a very good one. I've had some misfortunes, and twice I didn't get the money due me, because of dishonest assistants. And, I tell you truly, Patty, if I had lost five or six hundred dollars tonight, it would have been a hard blow. You have saved me from that, and I bless and thank you. Do you realize, little girl, what you are doing for me?"

"I'm so glad I can. Tell me about your sister."

"Clare? Oh, she is the dearest thing! She never has walked, but in spite of her affliction she is the happiest, cheeriest, sweetest nature you ever saw. I love her so, and I love to be able to get little delicacies and comforts for her. See, here is her picture."

Patty took the case and saw the portrait of a sweet-faced girl, little more than a child.

"She is a dear, Maude. I don't wonder you love her. Oh, I'm so glad I happened over here today. Do you know Bill Farnsworth?"

"I met him once or twice the same winter I met Chick Channing. Mr. Farnsworth seemed very stiff and sedate. Chick is much more fun."

"Chick is gayer, but Bill is an awfully nice man."

"I was with a vaudeville troupe that year. It wasn't very nice,—hard work and small pay. It was my last attempt on the stage. If I couldn't be a big and fine actress I didn't want to be any at all. So I'm glad I gave it up for this sort of work. This season is about over now, and I shall have entertainments in New York this winer. I've lots of influential patrons, and I hope for success. But I shall never forget your heavenly kindness in helping me out tonight. Now, perhaps, we had better be getting dressed."

Patty made a careful toilette, for she wanted to look her best, and she succeeded. The soft dainty white tulle was exceedingly becoming, and she had done her hair the prettiest way she knew. Maude's slippers were the least bit loose, but they looked all right, and Patty refused a loan of a pair of long white gloves.

"They're not wearing them with evening

[84]

gowns this season," she said, " and I hate them, anyhow."

" You're right," and Maude surveyed her critically. " Your arms are lovely,—so soft and dimpled. You are more effective without gloves."

Through the opening numbers of the concert, Patty sat in the ante-room waiting her turn. She was not nervous or apprehensive, and when the time came, she walked out on the platform and bowed gracefully, with a cordial little smile.

She was to sing almost exactly the selections of M'lle Farini. But she had substituted others in one or two instances, and, of course, for encores, she could make her own choice.

And there were plenty of encores. Patty's sweet voice charmed by its sympathy and grace, rather than by volume. And it made a very decided hit with the audience. They applauded continuously until Patty was forced to respond a second and a third time, after each of her numbers.

Channing, sitting in the audience, heard people saying, " Who is this Farini? I never heard of her before. Her voice is a little wonder!"

[85]

Miss Kent was delighted with Patty's success. She had felt sure the hearers would like Patty's music, but she did not expect such unanimous approval nor such enthusiasm.

Four times Patty was announced to sing, and as each was encored at least once, it made a good many songs. At the last appearance she was very tired, but she bravely endeavoured not to show it. She went through the number beautifully, but the deafening applause made it impossible for her not to give them one more.

" I can't," said Patty, as Maude came to her with entreaties. " I'm all in, as the boys say. Oh, well, I'll sing one more little thing. No accompaniment at all, please, Maude."

Then Patty returned to the platform and when the enthusiastic welcome ceased, she sang very softly a little cradle song. The haunting sweetness of the notes and the delicate languor of Patty's tired voice made an exquisite combination more effective even than her other work. She finished in a pure, fine minor strain, and with a little tired bow, walked slowly from the stage.

Then the house went wild. They clapped and shouted brava! and demanded more. But the concert was over; Miss Kent made a little speech of thanks, and the footlights went out. Reluctantly, the people rose from their seats, but hung around, hoping to get a glimpse of M'lle Farini.

" It isn't so much her voice," Chick overheard somebody say, " as the way she has with her. She's charming, that's what she is, charming! "

" We can't have supper in the dining-room," Maude said, laughingly, to Channing. " Patty would be mobbed. Those people are just lying in wait for her."

" But I want to," cried Patty. " I've done the work, now I want the fun. Let's have supper there. They won't really come up and speak to me, when they don't know me."

" Won't they! " said Maude. " But indeed you shall have supper wherever you like. You deserve anything you want. Come on, Chick, it's to be just as Patty says."

So to the supper-room they went, and there Patty became the observed of all. At first, she didn't mind, and then it became most embarrassing. She could hear her name mentioned on all sides, and though it was always coupled with compliments, it made her uncomfortable to be so conspicuous.

" Though of course," she said gaily, " they're

[87]

not talking about me, but about M'lle Farini. Well, I'm pretty hungry, Chick. Maude made me eat a light dinner, as I was going to sing. Now I want to make up. Can I have some bouillon, and some chicken *à là* king, and some salad, and some ice cream?"

"Well, well, what a little gourmande! Why, you'd have nightmare after all that!"

"No, I wouldn't. I'm fearfully hungry. Honest I am."

So Patty had her selection, and though she ate little of each course, she took small portions with decided relish.

"I feel like a new lady!" she declared when she had finished. "Is there dancing? Can I have a turn? I don't want to go to bed yet."

"Of course you can dance," said Maude. "But you must remain M'lle Farini for the evening. Can you remember?"

"'Course I can. It'll be fun. Besides, I'm only going to have one trot with Chick and then I'll go by-by, like a good little girl."

But, as might have been expected, after her one dance, Patty was besieged by would-be partners, clamouring for an introduction. The manager of the hotel was bribed, cajoled, and threatened in the various efforts of his guests to get introductions to Patty and to Miss Kent.

"Just one or two," Patty whispered to Maude, and so two or three young men won the coveted presentation, and Patty was urged to dance.

But this she refused. She wanted to chat a little with these strangers, but she didn't care to dance with men so lately made acquainted.

Channing acted as bodyguard, and his close inspection would have barred out any one he did not altogether approve of. But they were a nice class of men, polite and well-bred, and they were entertaining as well. Patty had a right down good time, and not the least part of the fun was the masquerading as another.

"You are staying here long, M'lle Farini?" asked Mr. Gaunt, an attractive man of musical tastes.

"No," Patty replied, "I have to leave early in the morning. I'm due to sing at another hotel tomorrow night."

"Ah, a near-by house?"

"Not very. Do you sing, Mr. Gaunt?"

"Yes, baritone. I'd like to sing with you. I've an idea our voices would blend."

"I'm sure they would. I love to sing duets. But," and pretty Patty looked regretful, "it cannot be. We will never meet again."

"How can you be so sure?"

"I feel it. But tomorrow I'm going to have my fortune told. If the seer says anything about our future meeting, then I'll look for you later on."

"If the seer is a true soothsayer, and no fake, he can't help telling you we will meet again; because it is a foregone conclusion."

"Then I shall expect you and look forward to the meeting," and Patty held out her hand to say good-night, for it was after midnight, and Maude was making signs for her to come with her.

But just then a clerk came toward them with a puzzled face. "There's a telephone call for a Miss Fairfield," he said; "and the speaker says she's here with Mr. Channing. Are you Mr. Channing, sir?"

"Yes," said Chick. "It's all right. M'lle Farini has occasion to use different names in her profession. Which booth?"

"This way, sir."

Channing, beckoning to Patty, followed the man, and whispered to her to take the message,

[90]

as it must be from some of the Freedom Castle people.

Patty went into the booth, and to her surprise was greeted by Philip Van Reypen.

"Well," she exclaimed, a little annoyed, "is this a habit? Do you expect to call me up every night at midnight?"

"Now, Pattykins, don't get mad. I called you up to apologize for what I said last night. I take this hour, 'cause I know you're all wrapped up in people all day, and only at night do you have a moment to waste on me, and I *must* tell you how sorry I am that I was rude to you."

"Rude, how?"

"Why, telling you I was coming up there whether you asked me or not. You don't want me to, do you?"

"No, Phil, since you ask me plainly, I *don't*. Not but that *I'd* like to see you, but I'm here on Bill Farnsworth's invitation, and since he didn't ask you,——"

"Yes, I know. And it's all right. I don't want to butt in where I'm not asked. And I'm sorry I called you up, if it bothered you. And——"

[91]

"All right, Phil. Now if you've any more to say, can't you write it? For I'm just going to bed. Good-night." And Patty hung up the receiver.

CHAPTER VII

THE FORTUNE TELLER

NEXT morning Patty and Maude had a cosy little breakfast in the latter's apartment, and then, arrayed in her riding habit, Patty went down, to find Channing waiting for her on the veranda.

"Good morning, M'lle Farini," he said gaily, "ready for a ride? Come along with us, won't you, Maude?"

"No, thank you, Chick. I'm not altogether certain that Patty's friends will forgive this performance and I'd be afraid to see them. But, oh, I can't tell you both what it has meant to me, and I do hope you'll have no cause to regret it."

"Not a bit of it! I'll fix it up all right," and Chick looked very big and powerful. "If anybody goes for Patty, he'll hear from me! See?"

"But I do want to see you again, Maude," said Patty, as they bade farewell. "Shall you be here long?"

"Only two or three days, at most. I have another concert here tomorrow night, but I'm sure of my artists for that. Do ride over again, both of you."

"We will," promised Channing, and then the two cantered away.

"Here they come!" cried Daisy, as from the porch of Freedom Castle she spied the two equestrians.

Jim Kenerley was at the block to help Patty alight, and as she ran up the steps, Adele clasped her in a welcoming embrace.

"You dear child!" she said. "What an experience you have had. Sit down here and tell us all about it."

So Patty told the whole story, exactly as it had happened, and Channing added details here and there.

Everybody was interested and asked all sorts of questions.

"Is it a nice hotel?" asked Mona. "Did you have any fun after the concert?"

"There was dancing," said Patty, "but I was too scared, when people called me M'lle Farini, to enjoy it much. I wanted to get away. I'm

[94]

glad I did it for Miss Kent, but—never again!"

"If she's the Maude Kent I once knew, you had no business to have anything to do with her," put in Farnsworth, in a gruff voice.

"She's the Miss Kent Chick Channing knows, and that's enough for me!" retorted Patty, and a little pink spot showed in either cheek, a sure sign that she was annoyed.

"Well, shall we go to the hermit's?" said Elise, anxious to avert the impending scene. "What *do* you think, Patty, Kit has a tooth-ache, and can't go, after all."

"Toothache!"

"Yes, a bad ulceration. He sent down word by Bobbink, that pet bellboy of his, that we were to go on without him. The boy will show us the way."

"How ridiculous! Why not wait till tomor-row?"

"No, Kit says the hermit man expects us and we must go. You'll go along, won't you?"

"Yes, of course. Shall I change this rigging, —or go as I am?"

"Go as you are. It's time we were off. Roger and Mona have gone on ahead, but as they

[95]

went in the opposite direction, I am not sure they'll get there before we do."

" Those two have a fancy for going in the opposite direction," laughed Patty; " ever notice it?"

" Not being stone blind, I have," Elise admitted, and really the interest Roger and Mona had for each other became more apparent each day.

The Kenerleys declined to go on the hermit expedition, saying that they knew their " fortune," and had no reason for questioning the future. So the others started.

Channing took possession of Patty, and merely saying " which way? " he led her across the wide lawn to the indicated path through the wood.

Elise followed, with Bob Peyton, who greatly admired the pretty New York girl. Farnsworth and Daisy Dow brought up the rear of the procession, and Bobbink, the ever useful courier, showed the way.

" Mr. Cameron says for you to do jes' wot I says," he announced, evidently greatly pleased at his position of power.

" Go ahead, Bobbink," said Bill; " show us the way, but don't talk too much."

"Yassir. Dis way, ladies an' gempmun."

It was a beautiful walk, through the Autumn sunshine and forest shade. Now they crossed a tiny brook or paused to admire a misty waterfall, and again they found a long stretch of good State road.

And sooner than any one expected, they reached the shack.

"Dat's de place," announced Bobbink, and stood, pointing to the dilapidated shanty at the side of the road.

"Who'll go in first?" asked Patty; "I'm scared."

"I'm not," and Daisy stepped nearer and peered curiously in at the door.

"Come in, woman!" said a strange, cracked old voice, and there followed a laugh like a cackle. "Come in, each and all."

Daisy pushed in and Farnsworth stepped in, too, for he didn't altogether like the sound of that laugh. Then they all crowded in and saw the old hermit, sitting in a hunched-up position on a pile of rugs in the corner of the hut.

"Which one first?" he muttered; "which pretty lady first? All have fortunes, wonderful fortunes coming to them."

Patty's Fortune

The old man's garb was somewhat like that of a monk. A dingy robe was girdled with a hempen rope, and a cowl-shaped hood fell well over his brow. His face was brown and seamed and wrinkled with age, and he wore queer-looking dark glasses. On his hands were old gloves that had once been white, but were now a dingy grey, and he seemed feeble, and unable to move without difficulty.

But he was alert, doubtless spurred by the hope of getting well paid.

"You go first, Daisy," said Patty; "then we'll see how it works."

"All right, I'm not afraid," and Daisy extended her palm to the old man.

"Here, wait!" she cried; "don't touch me with those dirty old gloves! Can't I wrap my handkerchief round my hand?"

The hermit made no objection, and Daisy wound a fresh handkerchief about her fingers, leaving the palm exposed for the seer to read.

He began, in a droning voice:

"Pretty lady, your home is far away. You are not of this end of the country, but off toward the setting sun. You will return there soon, and there you will meet your fate. He awaits you there, a man of brain and brawn,—

[98]

The Fortune Teller

a man who has ambition to become the mayor of——"

"Hush!" cried Daisy, snatching her hand away from his gloved fingers; "Don't you say another word! That's a secret! I don't want any more fortune! That man's a wizard!"

Daisy moved across the room, putting all the distance possible between her and the seer. With startled eyes, she gazed at him, as at a world wonder.

"Pooh! That was a chance shot, Daisy," said Elise. "Let me try, I've no secrets that I'm afraid he'll reveal."

Nor was she afraid of the grimy old glove, but put her finger tips carelessly into the old fellow's hand.

"Pretty lady heart-whole," declared the hermit. "Some day pretty lady fall in love, but not today. Some 'nother day, too! Pretty lady marry twice, two times! Ha, ha!"

"Silly!" said Elise, blushing a little, as she withdrew her hand. "I hate fortune telling. Next."

Patty, a little reluctantly, surrendered her hand to the seer, who took it lightly in his own. "Pretty lady all upset," he began. "So many suitors, all want pretty lady. But the fates have

[99]

decree! The lady must marry with the—"
he drew his hand across his eyes,—"I cannot
see clearly! I see a cat! Ha, no! I have it!
the pretty lady must marry with the Kit, ha,
yes; the Kit!"

"Good gracious!" exclaimed Patty, laughing,
"have I really got to marry Kit! Kit who?"

"That the wizard cannot tell. Only can I
read the name Kit. It is written in the lady's
fate."

"But s'pose I don't want to? S'pose I don't
like Kit as much as somebody else?"

"That makes nothing! It is fate. It may
not be denied."

"Well, all right. But I don't care so much
about my future husband. He's a long way
off. Tell me what will happen to me before he
arrives."

"Many adventures. You will today receive
a letter——"

"Goodness, I get letters every day! Any
particular letter?"

"Yes, a letter from one you love."

"Ah, Daddy, I expect."

"Nay, 'tis a younger man than your honourable parent. Then, soon the pretty lady will
inherit fortune."

The Fortune Teller

"Now, that's more interesting. Big fortune?"

"Oh,—my, yes! Large amount of moneys! And a journey,—a far journey."

"I don't care about the journey. Tell me more about the fortune. Who will leave it to me? Not my father, I hope."

"Nay, no near relative."

"That's good; I don't want my people to die. Well, anything more, Mister Hermit?"

"Beware of a dark lady——"

"Now I know you're the real thing!" and Patty laughed merrily. "I've been waiting for the 'dark lady' and the 'light-complected gentleman' who always figure in fortunes. Well, what about the dark lady?"

"If the pretty miss makes the fun, there is no more fortune for her," said the hermit, sulkily.

"I don't mind, so long as you don't take the money away."

"Tell mine, then," said Channing, as Patty resigned her place.

"You, sir, are an acrobat. You were employed in the Big Circus, the Hop—Hippodrome. When they discharged you, it was but

[101]

temporary. Do not fear, you will regain your position there."

"Why, you old wiz! How did you know that!" and Channing stared in pretended amazement; "I thought that episode in my career was a dead secret!"

"No episodes are secrets to me," declared the hermit. "Shall I tell further?"

"No, I guess that will be about all," and Channing moved quickly away from the strange old man.

Bob Peyton declined to have his past exposed to the public gaze; and he said he didn't care to know what the future held for him, he'd far rather be surprised at his life as it happened. So Bill Farnsworth was the next to test the wizard's powers.

"Big man," said the hermit, solemnly, as he scanned the broad palm Bill offered for inspection. "Big man, every way; body, heart, soul,—all."

"Thanks," said Farnsworth, "for the expansive if ambiguous compliment. Be a little more definite, please. What am I going to have for dinner today? Answer me that, and I'll believe in your wizardry."

"Big man is pleased to be sarcastic. The hermit does not waste his occult powers on foolish questions. In a few hours you will know what you will have for dinner. Why learn now?"

"Why, indeed? All right, old chap, tell me something worth while, then."

"That will I, sir! I'll tell you your fate in wedlock. You will yet wed a lovely lady, who, like your noble self, is of the Western birth. She is——"

"Drop it, man! Never mind what she is! Let me tell you what you are! Friends, behold Mr. Kit Cameron!" With a swift movement, Farnsworth drew off the old gloves from the hand that held his, and exposed the unmistakable slim white hands of the musician, Kit.

"Oh, you fraud!" cried Patty. "I half suspected it all the time!"

"I didn't," exclaimed Daisy. "You fooled me completely!"

"Oh, my fortune!" wailed Elise. "Where are those two lovely fates of mine?"

"And all my money!" groaned Patty. "I feel as if you had misappropriated my funds, Kit."

It had not been necessary further to remove Cameron's disguise, it was enough to see his hands, and hear his merry laugh.

"Hist!" cried Peyton, who had looked out

along the road. "Here come Roger and Mona. Let's give them a song and dance."

Kit drew on his old gloves again, and huddled into his crouched posture, just as the two came in at the hut's door.

"Just in time!" said Channing. "We've all had our fortunes told and were just about to go home. Take your turn now."

"I don't like to," said Mona, who was looking very happy and was blushing a little.

Keen-eyed Kit spied this. "Pretty lady," he began, in his droning tones, and as he also had a slight knowledge of ventriloquism, he most effectually disguised his own voice, "give me your little hand."

"Go on, Mona, we all did," said Patty, and wonderingly, Mona held out her hand.

"Never saw I the future so plainly revealed!" declared the seer. "'Tis written as in letters of fire! Lady, thy fate is sealed. It is bound up with that of a true and noble knight, a loving soul, a faithful comrade. I see the blush that mantles your rosy cheek, I see the trembling of your lily hand, I see the drooped eyelashes that veil your dancing eyes, and I see, stretching far into the future, years of happiness and joy."

The Fortune Teller

Kit released Mona's hand, and the girls crowded round her.

"What does he mean?" Daisy cried; "he spoke so in earnest."

"Stay!" and the seer raised his hand. "Now will I tell the fortune of the noble gentleman who but now arrived. Your hand, fair sir."

"Rubbish!" said Roger, disinclined for the performance.

"Go on, Farry," said Farnsworth, smiling. "We all did. Go ahead."

Roger gave over his hand, and the hermit rocked back and forth in glee. "Another clear writing of the fates!" he exclaimed. "I read of a happy future with the loved one. I read that only just now, within the hour, has the Fair said 'yes' to repeated pleadings, and the betrothal took place,——"

"Oh, I say!" and Roger tried to pull his hand from the hermit's grasp.

"'Tis a fair tale I read," went on the wizard, holding fast the hand he read; "two young hearts, made for each other, plighted by the singing brook—in the balmy sunshine—in a bower of roses by Bendemeer's stream—oh, hang it, old chap, let me be the first to congratulate you!"

[105]

Kit flung off his cowl with one hand, while with the other he gripped Roger's in a man-to-man grasp, and shook it heartily.

Then there was a small-sized pandemonium! The girls fell on Mona, kissing her and asking questions, while the men joined hands in a sort of war dance round Roger. Then they all made a circle round the engaged pair, and sang "Oats, Peas, Beans, and Barley Grows," with the zest of a crowd of children.

"Perfectly gorgeous! I think," cried Patty, as the excitement calmed down a little. "I sort of hoped it would be so, but I didn't expect it quite so soon."

"Neither did I," said Mona, shyly: "but, you see——"

"Oh, yes, we see," said Kit. "The picturesque spot,—the murmuring brook,—the whispering trees,—why, of course, you couldn't help it! Bless you, my children! and now, I want somebody to go out and get engaged to me. Who will volunteer?"

"Not today, Kit," said Patty, laughing. "Let troubles come singly for once. Today for this, tomorrow for yours. Come on, people, I can't wait to get home and tell Adele!"

CHAPTER VIII

A RIDE TOGETHER

ADELE was duly surprised and pleased to learn that Mona and Roger were engaged and declared they should have an announcement dinner that very night.

"Let's make it a real party," said Patty, "with a dance afterward."

"As if we didn't dance every night," said Elise, laughing. "But it will seem more like a party if we put on our best frocks."

"And decorate the table," added Daisy.

So the girls put their heads together to see what they could do in the way of effective and appropriate decoration.

"We might give her a shower," suggested Marie, after Mona had left the room.

"What sort of a shower? What could we buy and where could we buy it?"

"There's that little bazaar down in the village, but there's nothing decent there," said Patty.

[107]

"No," agreed Marie, "and we don't want to give Mona cheap little gimcracks."

"Well, we can't have a shower, that's out of the question," declared Daisy.

"But I *want* to have a shower," persisted Patty; "it will be no fun at all to give her a shower after we get back to New York. I'm going to invent some way to give it to her here."

"But there isn't any way———"

"Yes, there is, Daisy; now listen. Suppose we each give her some pretty trinket or thing of our own."

"Huh! Worn out old things!"

"No, of course not! But I've a little pearl ring that Mona likes awfully well, and I care a lot for it myself, too. So I think it would be a nice gift, just because I *do* like it myself."

"That's a good idea, Patty," said Adele; "I have a white and silver scarf that Mona just raves over. It's Egyptian, you know, and of some value. I think she'd like these things that we have personally used, quite as well as new things. You know Mona can buy anything she wants, but this personal note would touch her, I'm sure."

"Perhaps you're right," Daisy said, thought-

A Ride Together

fully. "I've an exquisite lace handkerchief I'd like to give her. It's one that was given to my mother by a French Princess."

"Oh, Daisy, you don't want to give that up."

"Yes, I do. I'm fond of Mona, and I'm glad for her to have it."

"I've a lovely fan," Elise said, "do you think she'd care for it? It's one of Duvelleroi's,— signed."

"Oh, she'd love it! We'll have a wonderful shower. What have you, Marie?"

"I can't think of anything worth while. Oh, yes, I have a centrepiece I'm embroidering for Christmas. It's a beauty, and I can finish it this afternoon, or, if I don't get it quite done, I can give it to her unfinished and put in the last stitches tomorrow."

"Capital!" and Patty smiled at the success of her "shower" plan. "What do you think, Chick?" she went on, as that individual, never very far from Patty's side, sauntered in, "we've the loveliest scheme!" And she told him of the shower. "I suppose you boys can't be in it, for Mona wouldn't want a jack-knife or pair of sleeve-links. And men don't shower engaged girls anyway."

"No, I suppose not. But what's the matter

[109]

with us men showering old Farrington? I'll bet he'd love to be showered."

"Oh, do!" and Patty clapped her hands. "Just the thing! Give him funny gifts, will you, Chick?"

"Of course I will. And I'll make the others come across, too."

Soon after luncheon, Patty had a telephone call which proved to be from Maude Kent. She begged Patty to come over to the hotel where she was, at once.

"Oh, I can't," said Patty. "We're getting up a party for Mona, she's just gone and got herself engaged to Roger Farrington, and we've got to do something about it."

"Well, you can come over for a short time. Truly, it's most important. Chick will whiz you over in a motor, and you can be back in two or three hours. What time is the party?"

"Oh, not till dinner time."

"Then come on. I want you terribly, and you'd want to come if you knew what for. I can't tell you on the telephone, it's a secret."

Chick was passing, and Patty beckoned to him. "Will you chauff me over to see Maude?" she asked, as she still held the receiver.

A Ride Together

"To the ends of the earth, if you've the slightest desire to go there, my lady fair."

"Well, all right, Maude. I'll come, but only for a few minutes."

"When do we start, queen of my heart?" and Channing bowed before her.

"In a few minutes. I'll scoot and dress, and you meet me here at three sharp."

"Your word is my bond. I'll be on deck."

Patty flew to her room and rang for the treasure of a Sarah. The girl was rapidly becoming a deft ladies'-maid, and when Patty merely said, "Rose Crêpe, Sarah," she took from the wardrobe the pretty afternoon gown of rose-coloured crêpe de chine, and went at once to get silk stockings and slippers to match, as well as the right hat, veil, and accessories.

On time, Patty stood again in the hall. Channing appeared, and at the same time Kit Cameron strolled in.

"Oh, Kit," said Patty, "however *did* you think of that crazy scheme of fortune telling?"

"My brain is full of nonsense, Patty, and sometimes it strikes out like that."

"But about my fortune? Did you just make it all up out of the solid? Or was there any——"

"Car's ready, Patty," interrupted Channing. "Leave that investigation till we come back."

"I don't want to," and Patty looked from one of the men to the other. "I want to hear about it now. I say, Kit, you drive me, instead of Chick, won't you?"

"Oh, now, that isn't fair!" and Channing looked decidedly annoyed. "You promised me, Patty——"

"No, I didn't. I asked you. That's quite different from promising. Now, don't sulk, and I'll give you an extra dance tonight."

"Two?"

"Well, yes, two, then, you greedy boy. Now run away and play."

"But is this all right?" said Kit, as he hesitated to take Channing's place.

"It doesn't seem so to me," Chick retorted, "But what Miss Fairfield says, goes!"

He turned on his heel, very much out of sorts at Patty's perverse ways, and as she saw the look on his face and the uncertainty on Kit's countenance, Patty broke into a laugh.

"Where are you going, Patty?" said Farnsworth, coming out of the house.

"Over to Poland Spring House, if I can get

A Ride Together

anybody to drive me. These boys are both unwilling. You drive me, Little Billee?"

Farnsworth looked at her a moment, with the expression of one who can scarcely believe his own ears. Then, just as Kit began to exclaim in indignation Big Bill took his place beside her and started the car.

"What possessed your kind heart to give me this pleasure?" he said, and his voice was so gentle it took from the words all suggestion of sarcasm or satire.

"The others were so tiresome. I don't think it's such a favour to allow a man to drive a car for you. Do you?"

"It depends on the man and the one who grants the favour. To me this is a decided boon. Do you realise, little girl, I never get a word with you nowadays? You never allow it. You're so wrapped up in Channing and Cameron, you've no eyes or ears for any one else."

"Oh, Little Billee, what a taradiddle! But when people don't believe what people say, people can't expect people to——"

"Wait! So many people get me all mixed up! And I do believe you, always. If I doubted your word about that telephone, it

[113]

was because I was misinformed. You see——"

"Yes, tell me how it was."

Patty was thoroughly enjoying herself. She had Big Bill where she wanted him, apologising for his abominable disbelief in her veracity. "Tell me who told you stories about me."

"Not stories, exactly. I wanted the long distance telephone that night, and when I went to the desk, the telephone clerk said you were using it, talking to a Mr. Van Reypen, and would I wait till you finished."

"And of course you thought I called Phil, whereas he called me! All right, Billee Boy, you're forguv."

"And then, he called you again, last night. Is this a habit of his?"

"Oh, Billee, that's just what I asked him. But how did you know he telephoned last night? Clerk again?"

"I was in the office, and as you weren't home, and the New York call might have been from your father, I answered. It was Van Reypen, and as he wanted to know where you were, of course I told him. Patty, what *did* he want? *Why* does he telephone you every night?"

"Well, let me see what he did want. He tele-

[114]

phoned last night, I believe, to apologise for telephoning the night before!"

"What nonsense!"

"Yes, he did! Don't you disbelieve me again!"

"Of course, I won't. All right, then, what did he say the first night, that he had to apologise for?"

"Oh, fiddlestrings, Billee, it was nothing of any consequence. I may as well tell you, though, he just wanted to be invited up here."

"Oh, he *did*, did he?"

"Yes, he *did*, did he! And I told him,——"

"Yes, Patty, what did you tell him?"

Patty turned her pretty head, and smiled full in Farnsworth's face. Her blue eyes were sparkling, her golden curls were tossed by the wind, her red lips wore a roguish expression, as she said, "I just told him I didn't want him."

"Patty! Did you really?"

"I sure did, Little Billee, but it wasn't quite true."

"What do you mean?"

"Well, you see, really, I *did* want him,—a little oh, only a *very* little,—but I knew *you* didn't and so I told him *I* didn't."

[115]

"Patty! what a torment you are!"

Patty's eyes opened wide. "Well, I like that! A torment! Because I headed him off for the simple reason that you don't want him! If that torments you, I'll telephone him tonight to come on!"

"There, there, Blue Eyes, take it easy. *I* don't want him, and *you* don't want him, and *we* won't have him! Now, let it go at that."

Big Bill smiled down happily at the flower-face that at first looked up at him a little angrily, and then smiled back.

"And now, Peaches, the Van Reypen incident is closed. Next, will you kindly tell me why you went in so strong for the Kent lady's concert?"

"Two reasons, Billee," said Patty, calmly. "First, and I hope most, because I was sorry for her, and wanted to help her out in her trouble. And second,——"

"Well?"

"Oh, because I'm a silly, vain thing, and I wanted to sing in public, and have people think I was Madame Thingamajig, and I like to have my voice praised,—and I'm just a little idiot!"

"You certainly are."

A Ride Together

"Why, Wil-yum Farns-worth! Aren't you ashamed of yourself?"

"Not half so ashamed as you ought to be."

"It isn't a crime to be vain of your accomplishments, and I owned up I was silly. Do you hate silly people?"

"Sometimes, not always. But look here, Patty, seriously, you don't want to be intimate with Maude Kent. She may be a nice girl, all right, but she has been an actress, and that is not the sort of people for you to associate with."

"I guess you don't know her very well, Bill; she is a noble self-sacrificing spirit, and she devotes her life to earning a living for herself and her mother and sister. I never knew a more devoted daughter and sister, than she is, and I adore her."

Farnsworth sighed. "I feared you'd fly off like that, Patty. You're so susceptible and impressionistic. But you must know that she is not the sort of girl you've been accustomed to know."

"So much the worse for the sort of girl I know, then. Idle, unoccupied creatures, thinking of nothing but the fleeting pleasures of the hour! Maude Kent is worth a dozen of them,

[117]

when it comes to nobility of purpose and energy of attainment. What do you know about her, Bill, that *isn't* admirable?"

"Only that, Patty. That she has been on the vaudeville stage. I met her personally only two or three times, and I took little interest in her. But I hate to see you grow fond of her. Are you going to see her today?"

"I am. But you need not see her. You can wait for me in the hotel parlour. I'm sorry I brought you."

"No, you're not, you're glad. And I'll not wait in any parlour. I'm going with you all the way."

As a matter of fact, Patty felt relieved, for she had no idea of what Maude wanted, and she feared it might be to sing again. This she had no intention of doing. Once was quite enough.

When they reached the hotel, they sent up their names, and Miss Kent came down. She received them in a small reception room, where they could be alone.

"You remember Mr. Farnsworth?" said Patty, after she had greeted Maude.

"Yes, indeed, very well. I'm so glad to see you again."

A Ride Together

Surely no one could criticise the gentle manner and soft voice, and Bill Farnsworth looked at her more kindly than he had intended to.

"And now, what's it all about?" asked Patty, when they were seated. "For, Maude, I must not stay but a few minutes. It's the night of the announcement party, and I've a lot to do for the affair."

"Very well, I'll tell you in a few words. Mr. Stengel, the manager, heard you sing here last night, and he wants an interview with you, with an idea of your going on the stage in light opera."

"What!" and Patty looked amazed, while Farnsworth bit his lips to restrain what he wanted to say.

"Yes; he says you have a delightful voice, but more than that, you have charm and a decided ability to make good in the parts for which he should cast you."

"Why, Maude, you must be crazy, to think for a minute that I'd consider such a proposition! I wouldn't dream of it, and I couldn't do it, anyway."

"Yes, you could. And I knew you'd feel this way, at first, but after you think it over——"

"Miss Kent," and Farnsworth's tones were

[119]

cold and incisive, "I know Miss Fairfield and her people quite well enough to speak with authority in this matter, and I assure you it is worse than useless for you to suggest such a thing."

"I knew it *would* strike you so at first, Mr. Farnsworth, and perhaps Patty's parents also. But I feel sure that if it were properly put before them——"

"Miss Kent," and Farnsworth rose, "there is no way of properly putting it before them. They would not even listen. And now I must ask you to excuse us. Come, Patty."

"But, Bill,——"

"Come Patty, at once."

"Must you obey him?" asked Miss Kent.

"She must," said Farnsworth, sternly. "Come, Patty."

"I must," said Patty, and with a strange look in her eyes, she rose. "I'll see you again about this, Maude," she said.

"She'll never see you again, about this, or anything else," Farnsworth declared, and his face was set and his voice hard. "Good day, Miss Kent."

"Good afternoon, Mr. Farnsworth. *Au revoir*, Patty."

A Ride Together

The two started home in silence. Patty's mind was full of conflicting emotions. The idea of going on the stage was so ridiculously unthinkable as to be of no importance, but the fact that she had been asked to do so filled her with a strange pride and satisfaction.

It was after a long time that Farnsworth said, gently, " Patty, you're so *many* kinds of a fool."

" Yes, sir," and Patty sighed, partly from relief that he wasn't going to scold and partly because she agreed with him.

" Now you see why I didn't want you to have anything to do with that Kent woman."

" Well, I don't see as she has done me any harm."

" You don't? Why, she has put that fool idea into your head. And you'll let it simmer and stew there until you begin to think that maybe it *would* be nice to go on the stage."

" Oh, Billee, I wouldn't do any such a thing! "

" No, not *now*, but after you mull over it, and especially if she ever gets hold of you again, which pray heaven, she never will."

" Goodness me! Little Billee, how would I look on the stage? Why, I'd be lost among all the big girls they have nowadays."

[121]

"You'd *look* all right, that's the worst of it. Now, see here, Patty, make me a solemn promise, will you? Not that you won't go on the stage, but that if you ever *think* of doing so, you'll tell me first. Will you promise me that?"

And Patty promised.

CHAPTER IX

THE "SHOWER"

THE announcement party was great fun. In every way it was made to seem like a formal party and not just the gathering of the clans.

Adele received the guests in the ballroom, with Mona by her side. Adele was gorgeous in her best evening gown, a rose-coloured velvet, and Mona, in white net, looked like a débutante.

Patty took especial pains with her toilette, though it was not entirely necessary, for Patty looked well in anything. She chose a white crêpe, whose bewildering masses of tulle ruchings veiled a skirt of silver lace. The bodice of silver lace was ruched and draped with the soft crêpe, and Patty's pretty throat and dimpled arms emerged as from a wave of sea foam. Her golden hair was massed in the prevailing fashion, caught with two pins of carved jade.

"Verra good, Eddie!" Patty remarked to

Sarah, as she viewed her completed self in the mirror.

"Miss?" said the maid, unfamiliar with Patty's nonchalant use of catch phrases.

"I said you done noble," Patty returned, absently, as she rearranged the jade pins. She wore no other ornaments, and catching up a long floating scarf of white tulle spangled with silver, she ran downstairs.

But, remembering the occasion, she made a most dignified entrance to the reception room, and bowed exaggeratedly to Adele. "So pleased!" she murmured, offering her finger-tips. "And Miss Galbraith. May I wish you all joy and felicity and happiness and good——"

"Come, come, Patty, give somebody else a chance. Don't babble your good wishes all night!" She turned to see Kit waiting his turn, and she laughingly gave way to him.

"Isn't it fine to see the men in their evening togs?" she exclaimed, turning to Elise. "I'm so used to seeing them in flannels or golf things, I scarcely recognise them."

"*Do* recognise me," implored Channing, "I'm the sweet young thing you promised three extra dances to."

"Three nothing!" returned Patty, carelessly. "I'm not sure I shall dance tonight, anyway. I shall spend my time admiring Mona, she looks so sweet."

Mona did look sweet. The occasion brought a look of shyness to her face, which was as becoming as it was unusual. Roger stood by, proudly gazing at her, as he was, in turn, congratulated and chaffed by the men.

Dinner was announced, and Jim Kenerley offered his arm to Mona, while Adele followed the pair with Roger. The orchestra played the wedding march, and Channing, who stood next to Patty, escorted her. The rotation of the table seats had been changed for the occasion, and Adele and Jim sat opposite one another with their guests of honour at their right hands. The others sat where they chose, and Channing deftly manœuvred to place Patty next to Kenerley, as he dropped into the chair at her left.

"Who's the great little old Machiavelli!" he said, chuckling. "Didn't I arrange that just about right! You see, if I put you next to Kenerley, you won't give *him* all your undivided attention, as you would, with any of the others."

"Well, if you aren't the piggy-wig!"

"I am, as far as you are concerned. I cheerfully admit it. And I've practically got you all to myself for the whole dinner time. You can't get away! Oh, joy!"

"Why is it such a feat? How do you know that I'm not equally crazy with joy to sit by you?"

"Oh, Patty! If I could believe that! What things you *do* say to a fellow! Do you *mean* it?"

"Considering I've only known you a few days, I couldn't really mean it. You see, I make friendships very slowly. Moreover, I never mean anything I say at dinner. Table talk is an art. I'm proficient in it, and I know the rules. And the first one is, never be sincere."

"Yes, I know that, too. But after dinner, say, out on that moonlit corner of the veranda——"

"There isn't any moon now."

"That's why I refer to it at the dinner table. I don't mean it, you see. Well, out in that unmoonlit corner, then, will you tell me one thing, —tell me truly?"

"Certainly. I'll tell you two things truly, even three, if you like. But they must be things of my own choosing."

"First, yes. Then it will be my turn. And I shall ask you something very important."

"Then I shall run away. My mind is so full of important things just now, that it simply won't hold another one."

"You don't know me yet. I'm a man who always has his own way."

"How interesting! I don't think I ever knew one before. All the men I have known have politely deferred to *my* way."

"Indeed? You must be longing for a change."

"Not only that, but it is positively necessary that I talk to my other-side man now. Where are your manners, that you have so long neglected your other-side lady?"

"With thee conversing, I forgot all manners. Also, the fair Miss Homer is absorbed in Mr. Peyton's gay chat."

"Well, give her a change, then. Marie, please turn this way. Mr. Channing is dying to talk to you."

Marie turned, with a pretty smile, and Patty gave her attention to Jim.

"You see, Jim," she said, "this is a formal dinner, and you must observe the fifteen minute rule. It isn't like our every-day meals.

Mona, how do you like being guest of honour?"

"I'm a little embarrassed," said Mona, who wasn't at all; "but I'm getting along somehow. Isn't Roger splendid?"

The naïveté of Mona's gaze at her newly betrothed made Jim Kenerley chuckle. "You'll do, Mona!" he said.

The table decorations were as appropriate as they could be made with little to work with. Patty had contrived a chime of wedding bells, of white tissue paper for the centrepiece, and at each plate was an orange, cored and holding a few flowers of various sorts.

"These are orange blossoms," Adele explained; "though not quite the conventional style, they show our good intentions."

The feast went on gaily, and after the dessert, the shower took place.

The head waiter brought in a tray on which were the gifts the girls had collected for Mona. They were beautiful and worth-while things, and the personal element they represented endeared them to the pleased recipient.

"You darling people!" she exclaimed. "You couldn't have done anything that would please me more! It is heavenly kind of you and I love you for it. I shall use them all, at once."

So Mona slipped Patty's ring on her finger, threw Adele's scarf round her shoulders, and tucking the wonderful lace handkerchief in her belt, she waved the fan to and fro. The centrepiece, which Marie managed to get finished in time, Mona calmly laid in place under her own dinner plate, and she declared that she was perfectly happy.

" Now, for *our* shower," said Jim. " It isn't fair that the bride-elect should get all the loot, so we take pleasure in presenting to our distinguished,—at least, distinguished-looking friend, and fellow-traveller, some few tokens of our approval of his course. Myself, I offer these dainty boudoir slippers, knowing that they will be acceptable, not only for their artistic merit, but for their intrinsic value. Take them, Farrington, with my tearful wish for your happiness."

Kenerley gave Roger a good-sized parcel, tied up in tissue paper and ribbons, which, when opened, disclosed a furiously gaudy and old-fashioned pair of " worsted-work " slippers. He had unearthed them at the bazaar in the village, where they had doubtless been on sale since the early eighties.

Everybody laughed at the grotesque things, but Roger, in the mood of the moment, made a gay and graceful speech of thanks.

Then Bob Peyton presented a smoking set. This was an impossible affair, of "hand-painted" china. The ash tray bore the cheerful motto of "ashes to ashes!" and the tobacco jar was so clouded with artistic smoke wreaths, that Kit declared it ought to be labelled "Dust to Dust."

Cameron's gift was a tie case. Evidently fashioned by feminine fingers, it was of pink silk, a little faded, embroidered with blue forget-me-nots.

"Tasty, isn't it?" said Kit, holding it up for general admiration. "I hesitated a long time between this and a sponge bag. The other would be more useful, but there's something so fetching about this,—that I couldn't get away from it."

"Don't let *me* get you away from it, Cameron," said Roger; "I'd hate to deprive you of anything you admire so sincerely. Take it from me——"

"No, Roger," said Kit, firmly. "I cannot take it from you. I give it to you,—a little grudgingly, 'tis true,—but I give it. I may

[130]

never have another chance to make you an announcement shower, and so, on this 'spicious 'casion, I stop at nothing."

"You're a noble fellow, Cameron," and Roger's voice was surcharged with emotion of some sort. " I accept your gift in the spirit in which it is given, and I trust I may some day have the opportunity to shower you in return."

" I hope to goodness you will, Farrington, and I now thank you in advance."

"Postpone those thanks, please," broke in Channing; "your time's up. I say, Old Top, here's the best prize yet. I offer you this picture frame. But it is no ordinary picture frame. Observe. It is made of birch bark in neat pattern, and decorated with real pine cones, securely glued on. No danger of their fetching loose, I've tested 'em. Now, in this highly artistic, if a trifle ponderous setting, you can place Miss Galbraith's portrait, and wear it next your heart or dream with it beneath your pillow. To be sure, it is pretty big and heavy for either of these uses, but's what a bit of inconvenience compared to the sentiment of the thing? "

Channing held out an enormous and cumbersome frame of heavy pine cones, glued to a board back; a fright of a thing, made by some of the native country people. As a matter of fact, these jesting gifts all came from the little village shop, where native talent was more in evidence than good taste.

"Heavenly!" exclaimed Roger, casting his eyes toward the ceiling. "Look, Mona, is it not a peach? Will you give me a miniature of your sweet face to grace it? Oh, *say* you will!"

Roger's absurd expression and exaggerated enthusiasm sent them all off into paroxysms of laughter, and Mona had no need for reply.

"Farrington, old man," said Bill Farnsworth then, "brace yourself. I have the best gift yet, for you. The most appropriate, and combining a graceful sentiment with a charming usefulness. Behold!"

From voluminous folds of white tissue paper, Bill shook out an Oriental robe, of gold-embroidered silk. It was really gorgeous and looked as if made for a Chinese mandarin. There were Dragons in raised work and borders of chrysanthemums. Bill flung it round Roger, to whose stalwart form the strange garb was most becoming.

Everybody exclaimed in admiration. Only

[132]

foolish gifts had been looked for and this was worthy of real praise. The long loose sleeves hung gracefully down, and the obi or sash was fringed with silk tassels.

"A stunning thing!" exclaimed Adele. "Where *did* you get it, Bill?"

"San Francisco," returned Farnsworth, "but my heart is broken. You have none of you noticed the real sentiment, the reason for the gift. Oh, how dense you are!"

"What do you mean?" asked Adele, puzzled.

"Can't you see?" cried Farnsworth. "Where are your wits? Why should I give that thing to Farrington, *today?*"

They all looked blank, till suddenly it dawned on Patty.

"Oh, Little Billee!" she cried, "oh, you clever, clever thing! Oh, girls, don't you see? It's a *Ki-Mona!*"

Then they did see, and they cheered and complimented Farnsworth on his witty gift.

"It's so clever and so beautiful, I think I shall take it myself," Mona declared, and Roger tossed it over to her. "With all my worldly goods—may as well begin at once," he said with a mock air of resignation.

The shower over, they went to the ballroom to

[133]

dance. Of course "Sir Roger de Coverly" was first on the programme, and after that the more modern dances.

Patty tried to evade Chick Channing, for he was growing a bit insistent in his attentions.

"Take me for a veranda stroll, Kit," she said, as she saw Channing approaching. "I want you to tell me all about that fortune business. But first, how did you ever come to think of it?"

"Oh, you know my fatal facility for practical jokes. Come, sit in this palmy bower, and I'll tell you all I know, and then some."

They sauntered in to the pretty glass-enclosed nook, and sat down among the palms. "You see," Kit went on, "I haven't played a joke in I dunno when, and I just *had* to get one off. So when I was prowling around, and struck that empty shack, the idea sprang full-fledged to my o'er clever brain. I fixed it up with Bobbink, —and the rest is history. Bobsy is a great boy, though a little fresh. He got the make-up for my face, and the rugs and things. He fixed them all in the old shanty, and then he carried out the toothache farce in accordance with my orders."

"Yes, he did very well. But I mean about

the fortunes. How did you know about the man Daisy is so interested in,—the one who wants to be Mayor of——"

" Sh! that's a state secret. I know lots of things, but I keep them to myself."

" All right," said Patty, seeing he was in earnest. " But about somebody leaving me money. Did you make *that* up? "

" Not entirely," and Kit still looked serious. " Perhaps you will receive a legacy some day. But did you note what I told you about your fate? "

" No," said Patty, as she ran away back to the house.

CHAPTER X

GOOD-BYE, SWEETHEART

THE days sped all too quickly at Freedom Castle. And on one golden, shining September afternoon, Patty realised that the next day they were all to go home.

"I don't want to go, Billy boy," she said, wistfully.

She was sitting in a swing that she had herself contrived, and Chick had achieved for her. It was a tangle of wistaria vine, pulled down from the great oak tree that it had climbed, and fashioned into a loop. This they had decorated with more sprays of the parent vine itself, and often Patty, or the others, added autumn leaves or trailing creepers or bunches of goldenrod or sumach till the swing was usually a rather dressy affair. One couldn't swing far in it, but then one didn't want to, and it was a charming place to sit.

Today, Patty, in a chic little suit of tan cloth, with a white silk blouse and a crimson tie, sat

[136]

Good-bye, Sweetheart

in the swing, disconsolately poking into the earth with her patent leather shoe tip.

"I'm sorry, Patty girl," and Big Bill looked regretfully at her. "But you see, the contract with the servants expires tomorrow, and they are all anxious to get away. You know, I've staid longer than I intended, now——"

"Yes, 'cause I begged you to," and Patty smiled at him. "Now if I beg you some more, will you stay some more?"

"In a min-nit! if I possibly could. But it's *un*-possible. You know I just came up for a few days to ratify the papers of transference and see to some business matters, and I've all sorts of important duties beckoning to me with both hands."

"But if I beckon to you with both hands——"

Patty held out her pretty hands, and slowly beckoned with each slender forefinger.

"Don't tempt me, you little witch. You know I'd do anything in this world for you, that didn't conflict with duty——"

"Wouldn't you conflict your duty—for me,— Little Billee?"

Patty's voice was wheedlesome, and her face was very sweet.

[137]

"*My* duty, yes, Patty." Bill looked stern. "But my duty to others,—no."

"Oh, Billee-ee-*ee*——"

"I'm sorry, dear, but I must disappoint you. My employers expect me in Boston tomorrow night, and I must not fail them."

"Well, can't we stay here, even if you go away? Jim and Adele could manage things, and we don't want servants. We could sort of camp out. I'm a good cook, and we'd have a lovely time."

Farnsworth considered. He looked far off and his fine brows knit as he thought over Patty's request. She looked at him and noted the cloud that came over his blue eyes as he turned to her, and said: "No, Apple Blosson, it can't be done. This place is a trust to me, in a way, and I'm responsible. I may not leave it to others. And I cannot remain myself. So there's no help for it, I must refuse you."

There was an air of finality about Bill's tones that told Patty there was no use in further coaxing.

"What's the matter, Patty?" he went on. "It isn't like you to tease so. I wish with all my heart I could give you what you ask, it hurts me worse than you know to refuse you anything. But I wouldn't be worthy of the trust reposed in me, if I failed in my duty."

"I hate duty," said Patty, petulantly; "it's a regular nuisance!"

"Gently, little girl, gently. What has happened to stir you up so? It's more than this ungratified whim of not staying here longer."

"What makes you think that?"

"I don't think, I know it. Why, Patty dear, I know every expression of your flower face, every look in your blue eyes, every droop of your sensitive mouth. And now it's drooping like a—like a, well, more like a perverse baby than anything else."

Farnsworth laughed gently as Patty's mouth suddenly curved upward in an involuntary smile, then, as it drooped again, she said; "I believe I'll tell you."

"Just as you think best. I wonder if you remember a promise you made me once."

"Oh, Little Billee, how did you know it referred to that?"

"Something seemed to hint it to me. Well, out with it. Are you still stage-struck?"

"No, but that manager, Mr. Stengel, won't give up the idea of putting me on in light opera. He says——"

"He says? Has he written to you?"

"No, Maude wrote me what he said. Any way, he thinks I have remarkable talent, and——"

"You haven't, Patty. Not remarkable talent. You have a pretty, light-weight voice, and a— h'm—shall we say an attractive appearance; but more than that is required for an opera success, even light opera. Forgive me, Apple Blossom, I know I am hurting your feelings, but it's better you should know the truth."

"Then why does Mr. Stengel want to put me into his plays?"

"He thinks you would look graceful and pretty and would be a drawing card for a time. Then, when your freshness wore off, as it would soon, he would throw you over like a worn-out toy."

"Well, *your* freshness hasn't worn off, Bill Farnsworth," and Patty stood up, her eyes dark with anger at his words. "And I don't care for any more of your opinions on a subject you know nothing about."

Big Bill Farnsworth smiled. "Well, was it a little ruffled kitten! Did it hate to be misjudged and misunderstood and all those horrid things! Well, then, Patty, see here. I'll let you off from your promise to tell *me* when you think of going on the stage, but you must tell your father. Though I can't think you would ever take such a step, without consulting him."

Patty's sudden blush and a guilty look in her eyes made Bill stare at her sharply, and then he said: "Oh, you *were* thinking of just that, —were you, Patty Fairfield? I can hardly believe it. You poor little thing, you *must* be infatuated! Is it all that Maude Kent's doing? Or, have you—Patty, you haven't *seen* Stengel, have you?"

"No," and Patty looked astounded at Bill's vehemence. "Why?"

"Thank heaven! I thought for the fraction of a second your infatuation might be for him. All right. You go home and talk to your father and your very sensible stepmother, and I'll warrant you'll forget this bee in your bonnet in pretty short order. And I hope you'll never see Maude Kent again. She has a certain charm and I don't wonder it appealed to a poor little innocent like you. Promise, Patty, you'll lay the case before your parents, before you take a further step."

"Of course I shan't go against their wishes,"

Patty spoke with great dignity, " but I know I can get them to see it as I do."

" Indeed? And just how do you see it? "

" Why, I see a fine and worthy career opening before me," Patty scowled as the grin on Bill's face grew broader, "a more valuable career than you are able to appreciate, a more— more——"

" Patty! Oh, you angel goose, you! *Do* stop, you'll finish me! " And Farnsworth threw back his head and roared with laughter. " And does this—er—valuable career shape itself to your clearer vision as being in the front row of the chorus, or farther back——"

Bill paused, stopped by the look of horror on Patty's face.

" Chorus! " she cried. " Why, you must be crazy! I shall be a prima donna, one of the reserved, exclusive ones, that nobody ever knows much about. I'm not going to have my picture all over the signboards, I can tell you that? "

" Nor the ash barrels? Well, for *this* relief, much thanks. Patty, I could laugh at you till I cried, but I feel more like crying first. I'm so sorry you've got this whimsey, for I know you'll hang on to it, like a puppy to a root;

and I shan't be here to look after you. But your father will do that."

"Why, where are you going?"

"West again. I don't know just when, but very soon. Now, it may be better for you to have this violently and get over it quicker, like mental measles. But unless you promise me faithfully to tell it all,—every word,—to your father and mother, I'll write them myself, all about it. Do you want me to do that?"

"Chick thinks it would be great fun for me to have a try at the stage."

"Did Channing say that?" Bill's face grew dark. "Did he, really, Patty?"

"Yes, he did. He said I'd make a screaming hit."

"Chick's only joking; don't let him fool you."

"No, he wasn't joking, and you know it. He thinks, as I do, that such an experience would broaden me——"

"Patty, stop! Do you want to be 'broadened' at the expense of all your refinement, your loveliness, your dainty girlhood, your fresh sweet youth,—oh, Patty, my little Patty, listen to me! If you never speak to me again, if you scorn me utterly, at least take my word for this, you must not, you *shall* not, think of this

[143]

thing! Patty, come to me, instead. Come to me, dear, let me take care of you, and find pleasures for you that will make you forget this foolishness——"

"It is not foolishness, but your talk is. I don't care to hear any more."

"Wait, dear, wait a moment. You know I love you, Patty, more than life itself; marry me, and let me teach you to forget this whim of yours——"

"It isn't a whim. And I don't *want* to marry you. This idea of mine is not a whim,—but a career, a splendid opportunity that calls to me—that promises wonderful things,—that——"

"Patty," and Farnsworth's face was white, "is that true,—what you said just now, that you—you don't *want* to marry me?"

"Yes, it's true," and Patty's angry blue eyes met his own sad ones.

"Then, that's all, Apple Blossom. You may go now. I've no fear that you will do anything further in this other matter, without your father's knowledge and no fear that he will allow it. So that's all right. Good-bye—Sweetheart!"

"Good-bye," and Patty flounced off. Yes,

Good-bye, Sweetheart

flounced is the word, for angry and chagrined, she let go of the swing she was holding, with a quick push, and whirling about, walked quickly toward the house.

The next morning the whole party left for New York.

"It's been perfectly lovely," Adele said to Farnsworth; "and if it were not for my baby girlie, I'd like to stay another week. But I hear her calling me!"

At Boston they were to stay over night. The party really broke up there, for several of the men were going in different directions.

But Adele gathered her brood of girls under her wing and carried them off to a hotel. And in the hotel lobby good-byes were said.

"I've had my long-feared telegram," said Farnsworth, "and I have to go to Arizona at once. Wasn't it lucky it didn't come before we left our happy hunting grounds?"

"Yes, indeed," said Adele, "it's been a beautiful party, Bill, and we just love you for giving it to us. Don't we, girls?"

"Yes!" they chorused, and laughingly interrupting their thanks, Farnsworth shook hands with everybody in hasty farewell.

Somehow, Patty was the last, and as he held out his hand to her, a gay voice was heard calling out, "Oh, here you are, people! How do you all do?"

They looked up to see Philip Van Reypen's smiling face, as he cordially greeted one after another.

"The most perfect time," Mona was saying, when Daisy caught her up; "Oh, yes, the *most perfect* time! What do you think, Phil, we had an engagement up there! A real live engagement! Guess the guilty parties!"

"Guess us!" exclaimed Roger, taking Mona's hand and looking mock sentimental.

"There's no use," said Daisy, "you can't get a rise out of them! They forestall you every time!"

"Congratulations, all the same," said Van Reypen, cordially. "Patty, how are you? Sunburned? Not very much." His manner was so cheery and his chatter so gay, nobody could be very serious, and the farewells became short and perfunctory.

Roger and Elise were taking Mona with them to Newport, where Mrs. Farrington was, and Bob Peyton was going directly home.

"Well," said Van Reypen, "it's lucky I came

along, Mrs. Kenerley, to help you care for your charges. Cameron, you and I must look after things."

"I'm on the job, too," said Channing. "You can't shake me till the last bell rings. Your train time, Farnsworth! So long, old man. See you when you return. You're always turning and returning. And all thanks for a bully time!"

"Good-bye, everybody," cried Bill, in his most genial way. "Glad you enjoyed it, and hope we can try it again some time. Good-bye, Patty," and with a swift hand-clasp, and a quick look in her eyes, Bill swung off and was lost to sight in the crowd.

Something seemed to snap in Patty's heart. A cloud swam before her eyes, and she swayed a little where she stood.

"All right, girl," said a strong, calm voice in her ear, and Van Reypen grasped her elbow and steadied her. Immediately, she was ashamed of her passing emotion, and laughed gaily, as she met his eyes.

"I'm here," he said simply; "you'll be taken care of."

"Wherever *did* you drop from?" and Patty

[147]

suddenly realised the queerness of his presence.

"Oh, I'm the little busybody who finds out things. I found out what train you people came down on, and I met it. Or rather, I tried to, but I reached it just as you left the station for this hostelry, so perforce, I followed you up. Now, may I attach myself to your cortège, Mrs. Kenerley? I can make myself useful, I assure you. Are you staying here over night?"

"Some of us are," replied Adele, who liked Phil, and was glad to see him.

"Then be my guests for the evening. We'll have dinner in great shape, and do a show, and just round up Boston generally."

The Kenerleys agreed, and soon the festivities began by the party sitting down for afternoon tea in the hotel tea room.

Daisy told Phil of Patty's escapade enacting the singer, M'lle Farini.

"What a lark!" said Van Reypen. "But I daresay you gave the audience a greater treat than if the lady herself had been there."

"Sure she did!" declared Channing. "I tell you, we'll see Patty on the stage yet. And a charming prima donna she would make, too.

I believe it would be a great success. Farnsworth says——"

But then some interruption occurred and the sentence was never finished.

In the evening, they all went to see a new light opera that was exceedingly popular. It was a dainty, pretty piece of foolery, full of Dresden china-looking ladies, and knights in theatrical armour, and the principal singer was a slight fairy-like person, much like Patty herself.

"You could give that Diva cards and spades," declared Chick, as they discussed her at an after theatre supper. "Why, Patty, you're more of an actress than she is, this minute."

"And a thousand times better-looking," said Philip.

"Bill Farnsworth says I'm good-looking enough," began Patty, slowly, and then she stopped short and changed the subject. She wanted to think it out for herself, before there was any more talk about it. So, if any one recurred to the matter, she quickly spoke of something else, and the evening passed merrily away.

CHAPTER XI

A BUBBLE BURST

ONE afternoon, about a week later, Philip Van Reypen called at the Fairfields home in New York. Being informed that Patty was out, he asked to see Mrs. Fairfield, and Nan received him in the library.

"So sorry Patty isn't here," she said, as she greeted him cordially. "She'll be sorry, too."

"Perhaps it's just as well," returned Philip. "I'd like a little talk with you. Look here, Mrs. Nan, has Patty said anything to you about going on the stage?"

"Unless you mean a Fifth Avenue stage, she certainly has not," and Nan smiled at the idea.

"No, don't laugh, it's serious. You know I met the crowd coming down from Maine, at Boston, and I was with them one evening. Well, they talked,—jestingly, it's true,—but they talked about Patty being in light opera some time,——"

"Why, Philip, how perfectly ridiculous! It was entirely a joke, of course."

[150]

"I don't think so. It seems, as near as I can make out, that Farnsworth put her up to it."

"Bill Farnsworth! Oh, I can't think he would."

"Well, Patty herself said to me that Farnsworth said she was good-looking enough, and then, somehow, she got mixed up with a singing-person of some sort, who used to be an actress. Farnsworth knew her in San Francisco, I believe. And she infatuated Patty to such an extent that——"

"I never heard such nonsense! Why hasn't Patty told me all this?"

"That's just the point. If there were nothing to it, she would have told you. That's why I fear she has taken the notion seriously."

"I can't think it yet. I'll ask her when she comes home."

"I'm not sure that would be wise. Why don't you wait, and see if she does anything in the matter. Elise Farrington said that a manager had asked to see Patty regarding the subject."

"A manager!" Nan fairly gasped. "Why, this is awful! What would her father say?"

"But wait a minute, let's look at the thing rationally. You know how susceptible Patty is to a new idea or a new influence. I think this ex-actress had bewitched the child, and to chide her would only make her more determined to stand by her new friend. Why not deal more diplomatically. Watch Patty, and if she does anything queer or inexplicable, follow it up, and see what it means. Of course, you know, Mrs. Nan, that I'm actuated only by honest interest in Patty's welfare."

"Oh, I know that, Philip; and I'm very glad you came to me with this story first. Perhaps it won't be necessary to speak of it to Mr. Fairfield, at least, not yet. He's busy, and a little bothered just now with some business matters; and if I could straighten out this foolishness without letting it worry him, I'd be glad."

"We'll do it," and Phil spoke heartily. "We'll save that little goosie from herself. Of course, you know, I worship the ground she walks on, and I'm going to win her yet. You think I've a chance, don't you?"

"I don't see why not, Phil. There's nobody I'd rather see Patty marry than you, but she is determined she won't listen to such a thing yet. She says she has too much fun being a belle, to tie herself down to any one man. And perhaps she is right. She's only twenty, and while that's quite old enough to marry, if she wants to, yet it's young enough to wait a while if she prefers."

"I quite agree to that. It's only that I want to be on the spot when she does make up her mind to marry. Of course she will, eventually."

"Of course. And you have every chance. Now, as to this other matter, do you think Mr. Farnsworth instigated the idea?"

"I gathered that from different things that were said. And the actress person was his friend. And I know that he took Patty over to Poland Spring House to see her."

"What's her name?"

"Kent,—Maude Kent. They call her Maudie."

"Queer Patty hasn't mentioned her. I agree with you, that looks as if she took the thing seriously."

"Oh, perhaps not," and Philip rose to go. "It may be I exaggerate the danger. But I'm so fearful of that capricious nature of hers,— you never can tell what whim she'll fly at next."

"That's true, and I'm so much obliged to you for putting me on my guard."

Nan said nothing to her husband on this subject, but she watched Patty more carefully. She was clever enough not to let the super-vision be apparent, but it was unremittent.

However, nothing transpired to rouse her sus-picions in any way. Patty was her own gay, sunny self, planning all sorts of gaieties and em-ployments for the winter season. She had by no means given up or neglected her club, that was for the purpose of giving pleasure to shop-girls or other working women, and she thought up plans for raising money for that philanthropic purpose.

She kept up her membership in the Current Events Club and in the Musical Society to which she belonged, and she showed no undue interest in the new light operas that were suc-cessively put upon the stage. She attended most of these, but she had always had a liking for them and that did not seem to Nan a spe-cial indication of histrionic intent.

But one evening, as the three Fairfields sat at dinner, Patty was called to the telephone. She left the table and after a time returned with sparkling eyes and rosy cheeks.

"Dear people," she said, smiling at her par-ents, "I've a surprise to spring on you. Will you be astounded to learn that your foolish

[154]

little Patty had a chance to make good in the world? To have a career that will mean fame and celebrity."

Nan almost choked. An icy hand seemed to clutch at her throat. The hour had struck, then. And with all her watchfulness she had not succeeded in preventing it!

"It perfectly wonderful," Patty was rattling on, "you can hardly believe it,—I hardly can, myself, but I'm going to be a great singer."

"You're that now, Kiddie," said her father, who had no idea of what lay back of this introduction.

"Yes, but more than that! Oh, Nan, it's too glorious! Daddy, what *do* you think? I'm going to sing in light opera!"

"You've often done that," he returned, thinking of her amateur performances. "One of your favourite Gilbert and Sullivan ones, or more modern this time?"

Patty laughed happily. "You don't get it yet, Dadsy. I mean in a real opera, on the real stage."

"What! Just say that again! My old ears must be failing me."

"I'm going to be a real prima donna! On the stage of a real theatre!"

"Not if I see you first. But elucidate this very extraordinary statement."

"I will." But even as she began to speak, Patty caught sight of Nan's face, and the lack of sympathy, nay, more, the look of positive disapproval she saw there, made her pause a moment. Then she went on, a little defiantly, "I suppose it will strike you queer at first, but you'll get used to it. Why, Dads, I found out, while I was up in Maine——"

"Down in Maine," corrected her father.

"Well, any old way to Maine, but I discovered that I have a voice! and more, I have a knack, a taste, a talent, even, for the stage. And,—I'm going to devote my life to it."

"Devote your life to it!" And Mr. Fairfield's tone was scathing. "If you're so anxious for a life of devotion, I'll put you in a convent. But on the stage! Not if the Court knows herself!"

Patty smiled tolerantly. "I was afraid you'd talk like that at first. It shall now be my duty and my pleasure to make you change your intelligent mind. Nan, you'll help me, won't you?"

Patty asked this with some misgiving, for Nan did not look entirely helpful.

A Bubble Burst

"Help you to go on the stage?" was the smiling retort, for Nan quickly decided to keep the discussion in a light key, if possible. "Yes, indeed, after some reputable physician has signed a certificate of your lunacy,—but *not* while you're in your right mind."

"Now, Nancy, don't go back on me! I depend on you to talk father over, though he won't need much argument, I'm sure."

"Look here, Patty," and her father spoke seriously; "tell me just what you're driving at."

"Only this, Dad. I've a chance to go on the stage in a new light opera and I want to go."

"Whose opera?"

"Do you mean the composer?"

"I do not. I mean the manager or owner, or whoever is getting you mixed up with it."

"Well, the manager is Mr. Stengel——"

"Stengel! Why, Patty, he's a—a *real* manager!"

"That's what I said," and Patty beamed at him. "And he is coming here tonight to see me,—to see *us* about it."

"Coming here!"

"Yes, don't be so overcome. You didn't

[157]

know your little goose girl would turn out a swan, did you?"

"But there's a misapprehension somewhere. You see, Mr. Stengel is *not* coming here to-night."

"Yes, he is, I've just telephoned that he might."

"You telephoned Stengel!"

"Well, not directly to him, but I told my friend, Miss Kent, that she might bring him."

"Who? What friend?"

"Miss Kent. I met her up—down in Maine. She's a musical—oh, Daddy Fairfield, *don't* look as if you'd been struck by lightning!"

"But I have, and I'm trying to crawl out from under the débris. Now the first thing you do, my child, you fly back to that telephone, and call off that little engagement for this evening. Tell your Maine friend that circumstances over which you have *no* control make it impossible for you to receive her and the illustrious manager this evening."

"But, Father,——"

"At once, Patty, please."

Mr. Fairfield spoke in a tone that Patty had not heard since she was a little girl, but she

[158]

well remembered it. She rose without a word and did as she was bid.

"Be very gentle with her, Fred," Nan murmured, as soon as Patty was out of hearing.

"I will," and Mr. Fairfield flashed a glance of amused understanding at his wife. "Did you know about this thing?"

"Only vaguely. I'll tell you some other time. But quash the scheme decidedly, won't you?"

"*Rather!*"

Patty came back, her face a little flushed, her lips a little pouting, but quite evidently ready for the fray.

"I did as you told me, Father," she began, "but I think you'll be sorry for the stand you've taken."

"Perhaps so, girlie, but I don't want my sorrow to interfere with my digestion. So let's drop the whole subject till after dinner."

It had always been a rule in the Fairfield household never to discuss unpleasant subjects at table. So Patty tacitly agreed and during the rest of the meal there was only gay conversation on light matters.

"Now, then," said Mr. Fairfield, when dinner was over, and the three were cosily settled in the pleasant library, "tell me over again and tell me slow."

And so, quietly, but still with that air of determination, Patty told about Maude Kent, and the concert at Poland Spring and how Mr. Stengel was interested and wanted to see her with a view to starring her in light opera.

Mr. Fairfield sighed, for he foresaw no easy task in trying to persuade his wilful daughter to his own point of view.

"Patty, dear," he said, "do you remember when you were a little girl, I gave you a lecture on proportion?"

"I do, Daddy, and I've never forgotten it!"

"Well, put it in practice now, then. Can't you see that it is out of all proportion to think of an ignorant, untrained girl like you stepping all at once into the rôle of a successful prima donna?"

"But more experienced people than you think I can."

"No, they don't, dear. This manager knows your limitations, he knows you have no stage lore or experience, and if he wants you, it is only because of your dainty and charming personality, and because there is a certain prestige in the fact of a society girl going on the stage.

A Bubble Burst

But, as soon as the novelty was over, he would fling you aside like a worn-out glove."

"How do you know? You never were a manager?"

"Patty, men of experience in this world don't have to adopt a profession to know many salient points regarding it. I shall have to ask you to take my word that I do know enough of managers and their ways to know my statement is true. Nor are the managers altogether wrong. It is their business to get performers who interest the public, and they have a right to use their efforts toward that end. But I don't want my daughter to be sacrificed to their business acumen. Now, will you drop this wild scheme without further argument, or shall we thresh it out further?"

"Why, I've no intention of dropping it, Dad," and Patty looked amazed at the idea.

"Oh, Lord, then I suppose we must go through with the farce. All right, go back to the telephone and have the Stengel man come, right here and now."

"May I? Oh, Dadsy, I knew you'd give in!"

"Give in nothing! I want to show you what a little ninny you are."

"Wait a minute," said Nan, as Patty rose

[161]

and walked toward the telephone table; "suppose we don't ask Mr. Stengel, at first,—but just have Miss Kent come and tell us about it."

"Good!" agreed Mr. Fairfield. "She can't come alone,—Patty, tell her we'll send the car for her. I'd like to go straight ahead with this interesting matter."

So Patty telephoned and Maude Kent said she would come. The car was despatched and in a tremor of impatience Patty waited for her friend's arrival.

The elder Fairfields made no further allusion to the subject, but talked on other matters till the guest was announced.

Maude Kent bustled in, and greeted Patty effusively, kissing her on both cheeks. She acknowledged introduction to the other two with gay cordiality, and seated herself in the middle of a sofa, flinging open her satin evening wrap. She wore a light-coloured gown, with a profusion of lace and a great deal of jewelry. Patty looked at her a little surprised, for she gave a different impression from the girl she had seen before. She couldn't herself quite define the difference, but Maude seemed less refined, louder, somehow, here in the Fairfield home, than she had in the big hotel.

And Patty wished she would act more reserved and less chatty and familiar.

"You see, Mr. Fairfield," Maude ran on, "we just *must* have our Patty in the profesh. We need her, and I assure you she'll make good."

"In just what way, Miss Kent?" asked Fred Fairfield, his keen eyes taking in the visitor's every move.

"Oh, she can sing, you know; and she's a looker, all right; and she has charm—oh, yes, decided charm."

"And is this enough, you think, to assure Mr. Stengel's giving her, say, a ten-year contract as a prima donna?"

"Well, hardly that!" and Maude laughed, heartily. "You men will have your little joke. But he would give her a good place in the chorus to start with, and doubtless Patty would work up. Oh, yes, she could work up, I feel sure. Patty is not afraid of hard work, are you, dearie?"

"And it is as a chorus girl that Mr. Stengel wishes to engage Patty?" Fred Fairfield's

[163]

voice was quiet, but his eyes shot gleams of indignation.

"Why, yes, Mr. Fairfield; she couldn't expect a higher position at first."

"And would she be assured of having it in time?"

"If she caught on with the public,—or, if Mr. Stengel took a liking to her personally——"

"That will do, Miss Kent. I'm sure you will forgive me if I decline to pursue this subject further. My daughter most certainly will not go into any venture of Mr. Stengel's, or accept any other position on the stage. The incident is closed."

There was something in Fred Fairchild's face that forbade the indignant rejoinder Maude Kent was about to make. And it was with a sudden accession of dignity that she rose to her feet and drew her wrap about her.

"Very well," she said; "it is closed. As a matter of explanation, let me say that my interest in the thing is a legitimately financial one. Mr. Stengel gives me a fair commission on the young ladies I persuade to join his chorus. As I am self-supporting, this means something to me. Moreover, I am personally fond of Miss Fairfield, and I am sorry not to

[164]

A Bubble Burst

have achieved the triumph of her consent. But since it is impossible, I can only bid you all good evening."

With the air of an offended queen, Maude Kent swept from the room, and the Fairfield chauffeur took her back to her home.

"Patty, you everlasting little goose!" said Fred Fairfield as he took his daughter in his arms, "forget it! There's no harm done, and nobody need ever know how foolish you were. Your bubble's burst, your air castle is in ruins, but your old father is still here to look after you, and laugh with you over your ridiculous schemes. Now, forget this one and start another!"

CHAPTER XII

MIDDY

"WHITHER away, Patty?" asked Nan, as Patty came downstairs one bright morning in late October, hatted and gowned for the street.

"I'm going out on multifarious errands. First, I shall make a certain florist I wot me of, wish he had never been born. What *do* you think? I ordered pink chrysanthemums and he sent yellow? Could villainy go further? And then I've some small shopping to do. Any errands?"

"No, unless you stop in at the photographer's and see if my pictures are done."

"All right I will. By, by."

Patty got into the big car, with its open top, and drew in long breaths of the crisp autumn air.

"To Morley, the florist's, first, Martin," she told the chauffeur.

As they drove down Fifth Avenue, Patty

[166]

nodded to acquaintances now and then. She was very happy, for she was planning a pleasant outing for her club of working girls, and it greatly interested her. She had long ago gotten over her foolish notion about the stage, and was now able to laugh at the recollection of her silly idea. But she occasionally sang at a concert for charity or for the entertainment of her friends, and her voice, by reason of study and practice, was growing stronger and fuller.

When she reached Morley's the florist's doorman assisted Patty from the car, and she went into the shop.

Though she had threatened to reprove him severely for his error about the flowers, Patty was really very polite, and merely called his attention to the mistake, which he promised to rectify at once. Then, selecting a small bunch of violets to pin on her coat, Patty went out.

The doorman, who had been looking in the window, to see when she started, sprang to attention, and then, as Patty stepped toward her car, she stood stock-still in amazement. For there, on the back seat, sat a smiling baby, a chubby rosy-cheeked child about two years old.

"Why, you cunning Kiddy!" exclaimed Patty,

"where in the world did you come from? What are you doing in my car?"

The baby smiled at her, and holding out a little white-mittened hand, said: "F'owers? F'owers for Middy?"

"Who is she, Martin?" asked Patty of the chauffeur. "How did she get here?"

Martin looked around. The car was a long one, and he had not turned to look back since Patty went into the shop.

"Why, Miss Patty, I don't know! Maybe some of your friends left her?"

"No, of course, no one would do that, and besides, I don't know the child. Who are you, baby?"

"Middy," said the little one. "I Middy."

"You are, are you? Well, that doesn't help much. Who brought you here, Middy?"

"Muddy."

"Muddy, Middy. Your vocabulary seems to be limited! Well, what shall I do with you?"

The baby gurgled and smiled and reiterated a demand for "f'owers."

"Yes, you may have the flowers," and Patty gave her the violets, "but I don't understand your presence here."

Apparently it mattered not to the baby what

Middy

Patty understood, and she smelled the flowers with decided evidences of satisfaction.

Patty turned to the doorman, who had followed her from the shop.

"What do you make of it?" she said.

The man stared. "I don't know, ma'am. There was no baby in the car when you arrived here."

"That there was not," agreed Patty. "Well, how did she get there?"

"I'm sure I've no idea, ma'am."

"Weren't you here while I was in the store?"

"Yes, ma'am, but I was looking in at you, so's to be ready to open your car door as soon as you came out."

"Well, I never heard of anything so queer. I wonder what I'd better do."

"Shall I call a policeman, ma'am?"

"Policeman? Gracious, no! This is a nice child. See how pretty she is, and how well dressed."

"Yes, ma'am."

Patty looked up and down the street, but saw no one whom she could connect with the baby's presence. A policeman drew near, and his expression was questioning. He hadn't realised that there was a strange baby in the case, but he saw the lady was in a dilemma of some sort, and he was about to ask why.

But Patty jumped in the car beside the child, and said, "Home, Martin," so quickly, that the policeman wandered on without a word.

"It's ridiculous to take you home, baby," Patty said; "but what can I do with you?"

"F'owers," said the little voice, and the stranger offered them to Patty to smell.

"Yes, nice flowers," returned Patty, absently, as she stared hard at her visitor. "Who are you, dear?"

"Middy,—des Middy," and the little face dimpled in glee.

"Well, Middy, you're one too many for me!" and they went on toward home.

"Oh, Nan!" cried Patty, as she took her new friend indoors, "look who's here!"

"Who is she?" asked Nan, looking up from her book, as Patty deposited the small morsel of humanity on a sofa.

"Dunno. She was wished on me while I was in at Morley's. Came out of the shop to find her sitting bolt upright in the car."

"Really? Did somebody abandon her?"

"Can't say. She wasn't there,—and then, she *was* there! That's all I know. Want her?"

Middy

"Certainly not. But what are you going to do with her?"

The stranger seemed to sense a lack of welcome, and putting up a pathetic little red lip, said in tragic tones. "Middy 'ants Muddy."

"You poor little thing!" cried Patty, catching her up in her arms. "Did your mother put you there?"

"Ess, Muddy frowed Middy in au'mobile. Middy 'ant do home."

"Where is your home?"

The baby's face smiled beatifically, but the midget only said "Vere?"

"Don't you know yourself?" and the baby shook her head.

"It's clear enough, Patty, somebody has abandoned the little thing. How awful! And such a pretty baby!"

"And beautifully dressed. Look, Nan, see the little white kid shoes, and fine little handkerchief linen frock. And her cap is all hand-embroidered."

"And her coat is of the best possible quality. Look at the fineness of the cloth."

"Well, what about it?"

"I can't make it out. If it were a poor

[171]

child, I'd think it a case of abandonment. Oh, Patty, I'll tell you! Somebody kidnapped a rich child, and then they became frightened, and slipped her into your car to save themselves from discovery."

"Why, of course that's it! How clever you are, Nan, to think it out! For she is a refined, sweet baby, not a bit like a slum child."

This was true. The dark curls that clustered on the baby's brow were fine and soft, her little hands were well cared for, and her raiment was immaculate and of the best. But they searched in vain for any name or distinguishing mark on her clothes. Even the coat and cap had no maker's tag in them, though it was evident that there had been.

"See," said Patty, "they've ripped out the store tag! The kidnappers did that. Did the bad mans take you, baby?"

"No, Muddy b'ing baby. Des Muddy."

"Muddy is, of course, her mother. Now, we know her mother never put the child in the car, so I guess we can't depend on her story."

"Ess," and the little one grew emphatic. "Muddy did b'ing Middy. An' Muddy *did* put Middy in au'mobile."

"Well, I give it up. She seems to know what she's talking about, but I do believe she was kidnapped. We'll have to keep her for a day or two. It'll be in the papers, of course."

"Perhaps she's hungry, Nan; what ought she to eat?"

"Anything simple. Ask Louise for some milk and crackers."

But Middy did not seem hungry. She took but a sip of the milk and a mere nibble of the cracker. She seemed happy, and though she beamed impartially on everybody, she said little.

"She ought to have something to play with," decreed Patty. "There isn't a thing in the house. I ransacked the attic rooms for that last missionary box. I haven't any favours or toys left. Nan, I'm going to take her out to buy some, and maybe we'll meet her distracted mother looking for her."

"Maybe you won't! But go along, if you like. I'll go with you as far as Gordon's."

Putting on the baby's wraps again, Patty started off. The child was delighted to go in the car.

"Nice au'mobile," she said, patting the cushions.

"Hear her patronising tone!" laughed Nan. "Middy have au'mobile at home?" she inquired.

"No, no," was the reply as the tiny white teeth showed in a sunny smile.

"You're a lovely-natured little scamp, anyway," declared Patty, hugging the morsel to her, and Middy crowed in contentment.

Patty took her to a large toyshop. As they entered, a clerk came forward to wait on them. "What can I show you?" he asked.

"Wait a minute," said Patty. "Let the baby choose. Now, Middy, what do you like best?"

The child looked around deliberately. Then, spying some dolls, she made a rush for them. "Middy 'ant Dolly-baby! Ess!"

"Very well, you shall have a dolly-baby. This one, or this one?"

"No. 'Reat bid one! See!"

She pointed to the largest doll of all, a very magnificent affair, indeed.

"Oh, that's too big for a little girl like Middy! Have a dear little, cunning, baby doll."

But, no, the child was self-willed, and insisted on the big doll.

[174]

"Well," said Patty, "I suppose she might as well have it," so the big doll was put into the outstretched little arms, and peace reigned.

"An' a dolly vadon," the small tyrant went on. This was translated to mean dolly wagon, by the clerk, who was more versed than Patty in baby language.

"Good gracious, sister! You'll bankrupt me!" and Patty inquired the price of the little coaches.

Moreover, the wilful purchaser declined all but the best and biggest, and when it was ordered sent home, Patty hurried her charge out of the store lest she demand further booty.

With the big doll they went back home, and Patty set herself to work to get further knowledge of the child's antecedents.

But here efforts were vain. She learned only the age of her guest and no other statistics.

"Mos' two 'ears old," Middy declared she was, but except for that, no information was forthcoming.

Inquiries regarding her father brought only blank looks.

"Haven't you any father at all?" urged Patty.

[175]

"No; no fader. Poor Middy dot no fader!"

But the bid for sympathy was so clearly insincere, and the accompanying smile so merry that Patty concluded she had no father of her recollection.

It soon transpired that the wily mite called for sympathy on all occasions. "Poor Middy," was her constant plea, if she wanted anything.

"Poor Middy hung'y," she said at last, and this time she eagerly welcomed the milk and crackers.

"Now, Poor Middy s'eepy," she announced, when her meal was over, and willingly she allowed Patty to bathe her hands and face and put her to rest on the couch in the living-room.

"Did you ever see anything so pretty?" exclaimed Patty to Nan, as the latter returned. "She's been sleeping nearly two hours. See her little hand, just like a crumpled rose-leaf. What *will* Dad say?"

They let the baby sit up until Mr. Fairfield's arrival, anxious to know his opinion of the strange circumstance.

"Well, bless my soul!" he exclaimed. "Patty, what queer jinks will you cut up next?"

"But, Dads, it surely wasn't my fault! It was none of *my* doing!"

"Of course not, child. I expect you're one of those cut out for queer happenings. There are such people, you know."

"Well, but what do you think about it? How do you explain it? Do you think, as Nan does, that kidnappers put her in the car, because they were frightened for their own safety, if found with the little thing?"

"Not altogether likely. I think it's more probable the mother abandoned it."

"Oh, how could she! That angel child. She *is* a beauty, isn't she, Daddy?"

"Very pretty, very pretty, indeed. But a problem. The end is not yet, Pattykins. I'm sorry this has happened. There's been no kidnapping. If there had it would have been in the papers. This is, it seems to me, a deep laid plot of some sort. Well, we must await developments."

Patty went away with Louise to make the baby a bed for the night, in her own dressing-room. With pillows and some guarding chairs, they improvised a crib, and the process of undressing the baby proved such a gala time that the whole house rang with merriment.

As they took off one little white shoe, a folded paper dropped out. It was addressed to Patty herself,—but with a feeling of apprehension as to what it might contain, she ran downstairs with it, before she looked inside at all.

CHAPTER XIII

CHICK'S PLAN

"HERE'S a note," said Patty to her parents. "It was in the baby's shoe! I haven't read it. Open it, Dad."

Mr. Fairfield took the paper Patty handed him, and read aloud:

To Miss Fairfield:—Will you not adopt my little girl? I am a woman of your own class in society. I married my father's chauffeur, and my family disowned me. Now, I am in most unfortunate circumstances, but I have tried to keep my baby well-nurtured and well-dressed. I can do it no longer, and though it breaks my heart to give her up, I want her to have a home of refinement and comfort. You are rich, and you are devoted to charitable work. Will you not keep her for your own? Or, if you are unwilling to do this, will you not find a good kind friend who will take her? Her name is Millicent, but I call her Milly. She is a year and ten months old, and she has a lovely disposition. Do not attempt to seek me out. I will never try to see the child nor will I make trouble in any way about the adoption. Please keep her yourself.

From MILLY'S MOTHER.

P. S.—She loves custards and hates oatmeal.

[179]

"Well," said Patty, "here's a state of things! Mrs. Milly must think I'm anxious to start an orphan asylum? The kiddy is a dear,—but I'm not sure *I* care to adopt her."

"I should say *not!*" and Nan looked indignant. "I never heard of such nerve!"

"Now, now," broke in Mr. Fairfield, "the poor mother is not so much to be blamed. I feel very sorry for her. Think of the circumstances. She married the chauffeur,—ran away with him, likely,—and now he has doubtless deserted her, or worse, remained with her and treats her cruelly. Poor girl, it's only natural that she should want her baby to grow up in a home having the advantages she herself enjoyed. If I were you, Patty-girl, I'd try to find a good home for the little waif; that is, unless you wish to keep her here."

"No," replied Patty, thoughtfully, "I don't believe I do. You can't take a baby as you would a lapdog. There is a responsibility and a care that you would have to assume, and I'm sure I don't want to devote the better part of my existence to bringing up a child that doesn't belong to me."

"Of course you don't," agreed Nan. "The

Chick's Plan

idea is absurd. But the question is, who would take her?"

"I can't think of anybody," declared Patty, wrinkling her brows. "Could we advertise?"

"No," said Mr. Fairfield, "that wouldn't do at all. You'll have to keep the baby for a little while, and ask your friends if they know of a possible home for her. When it is noised around, I'm sure some one will come forward to want her."

"And meantime, Daddy, you can look after her! I'm planning a busy winter, and I've no time for stray lambs."

"Can't you get a nurse?" suggested Mr. Fairfield.

"Oh, yes," and Nan sighed. "But we've as many servants as the house will easily accommodate now; and a nurse and a nursery and the nurse's room will necessitate rearranging everything. It's no joke to introduce a baby member into a household, I can tell you!"

"You can keep my dressing-room for a nursery," offered Patty; "I can get along without it for a time."

"It isn't really big enough," objected Nan. "The child must have lots of fresh air, and— oh, I never *did* have any patience with those

[181]

idiot people who say, 'Why do women waste their affection on dogs? Why not adopt a dear little baby?' It's a very different proposition, I can tell you! Of course, we'll have to have a nurse, if the child stays here at all, but where we'll put her *I* don't know."

"Well," said Patty, hopefully, "perhaps we can find a home for her quickly. And, too, I'd like to have here here a few weeks. I think she's a darling plaything, but I don't want to keep her all her life. I wonder who the mother is. Do you suppose she knows me?"

"Of course she knows of you," said her father; "your name is often in the papers in connection with various charities as well as in the social notes. She chose you, probably, as being too kind-hearted to shift the responsibility of the affair."

"And I am! I'll accept the responsibility of finding Milly a home, but it can't be here, of that I'm certain."

"How shall you go about it?" asked Nan, looking helpless and rather hopeless.

"With energy and promptness," returned Patty. "And the promptness begins right now."

She seated herself at the telephone table and

called up a wealthy and childless woman of her acquaintance.

"Oh, Mrs. Porter," she began, "I've the most wonderful opportunity for you! Don't you want to adopt a baby girl, a real Wonder-Child, all big, dark eyes and curly hair and the sweetest little hands and feet?"

"Oh, thank you, no," replied the amused voice at the other end of the line; "it is, indeed, a chance of a thousand, I am sure; but we're going South for the winter, and we shall be bobbing about, with no settled abode for a baby. Where did you get the paragon?"

"I have it on trial, and I want to dispose of it advantageously. Don't you know of any one who might take her?"

"Let me see. I believe Mrs. Bishop did say something about some friend of hers who knew of somebody who was about to take a child from an orphan asylum; but I remember now, she especially wanted a blonde."

"Oh, but brunettes are *ever* so much nicer! I'm a blonde myself, and it's awfully monotonous! Do tell me the name of the friend's friend,—or whoever it was."

"I don't know, really. It was about a month

ago I heard of it. But Mrs. Bishop can tell you,—Mrs. Warrington Bishop."

"I don't know her," said Patty, "may I use your name as an introduction?"

"Certainly. And if I can think up anybody else I'll let you know."

That was but the first of a hundred similar conversations that Patty held. She used the telephone, as it meant far less time wasted than personal visits would consume, and she hoped each call would bring indirect results, if not immediate success. But everybody was too engrossed in society or philanthropy or some hobby or travelling about, to consider for a moment the acquisition of a new charge.

Two or three times there was a glimmer of a hope of success and Patty would go flying off to call on a possible client. But always it proved a vain chimera. One lady wanted a baby to adopt, but would only take a boy. Another was most desirous of an infant, but it must be not more than six weeks old. Another had intended adopting a child, but had suddenly turned to settlement work instead.

The days went by, and Patty became almost disheartened. Nan and her father tried to help

[184]

her, but they, too, met with no success. Mr. Fairfield spoke to several business friends of his, but they either laughed at him or politely expressed their lack of interest in the matter.

A nurse had been engaged, a skilled and capable trained nurse; for Patty argued that if they wanted to find a good home for Milly they must keep her in the pink of condition.

But though the nurse was most efficient, she was dictatorial and high-tempered, and her superior air offended the other servants, and caused Housekeeper Nan no end of trouble. They thought of changing the nurse, but Miss Swift took such good care of her charge that they continued to keep her.

The small cause of all the excitement went on her sunny-faced merry-hearted way, unknowing what turmoil she had stirred up.

" Middy lub Patty," she would say, toddling to Patty's side as she sat at her everlasting telephone conversations. " Middy fink Patty booful! "

" Yes, and Patty finks Middy is booful," catching the baby up in her arms, " but you are a terrible responsibility! "

" Fot is tebble spombilty? "

[185]

"Well, it's what you are. I don't know what to do with you!"

"Lub me," suggested Milly, twining her chubby arms around Patty's neck till she nearly choked her. "Tell me I's your pressus babykins."

"Yes, you're all of that; and, as a matter of fact, I'm getting too fond of you, you little fat rascal!"

"I must beg of you, Miss Fairfield, not to caress the child so much," said the cold voice of Nurse Swift. "It is conceded by all authorities that kissing is most harmful——"

"Fudge!" said Patty; "I'm only kissing the back of her neck. Microbes don't hurt back there. Do they, Doodlums?" and she cuddled the baby again, while Miss Swift looked on in high dudgeon.

"Of course," she said, primly, "if my advice, based on experience and knowledge, is not to be considered at all, it might be well if you employed some other——"

"There, there, Nurse," interrupted Patty, "we're not going to employ anybody else. Take the kiddy-wid, and put her in a glass case. Then she won't get kissed and cuddled by bad, naughty, ignorant Pattys. By-by, Curly-head!"

"No, no! Middy 'tay wiv Patty. Middy not go wiv bad Nursie!"

"Listen, Dearie Girl. Go away with Nursie now, and get nice bread and milk, and come back to see Patty some 'nother time."

This reasoning worked well and the baby went off smiling and throwing kisses back to Patty.

"Oh, me, oh, my," sighed Patty, "what can I do, what *can* I do?"

That evening Chick Channing called. To him Patty narrated her difficulties.

"Don't you know of anybody who wants a perfectly angel child?" she said. "Truly there never was such a little ray of sunshine, such a sweet disposition and intelligent mind."

But Channing didn't know of a single applicant for such a treasure.

"But I'll tell you what," he said; "let's peddle her. Tomorrow I'll come for you in my runabout, and you have the kiddy all dolled up fine, and we'll take her round from house to house and offer her to the highest bidder."

"There won't be any bidders," said Patty, disconsolately.

"Oh, I don't know. We can exploit her, and her appearance will be all to the good. Anyway, we can try it, and it'll give the poor little scrap an outing, if nothing more. And give her overworked nurse a chance for an hour off."

So Patty agreed, and the next afternoon Chick came for them. The baby looked a dream, in her white coat and hat, her clustering curls showing a glimpse of pink hair-ribbon.

"Where first?" asked Chick, as they started off in gay spirits.

"Mercy, *I* don't know!" returned Patty. "I thought you were running this scheme, and that you had places in view."

"Not I. But if you haven't either, I suggest we just stop, hit or miss, at any house that looks hospitable."

"Nonsense, we can't do that."

"Well, then let's take her to an orphan asylum or children's home and just leave her there."

"No, indeed!" and Patty clasped Milly close. "She shan't go to any such place! Why, they mightn't be kind to her!"

"Probably not. But what, then?"

"Oh, dear, I don't know. What good **are**

[188]

you, Chick, if you can't suggest something? I'm worn out pondering on the subject."

"Well, if it's as bad as that, I *must* invent something. Let me see. Oh, by the way, are you going to the Meredith tea this afternoon?"

"I meant to go, till you trumped up this plan, which, if you'll excuse me, is the biggest wild-goose chase I ever saw!"

"Not unless you're the wild goose. I assure you I'm not. And to prove it, here's a plan. Let's go to the tea, and take this little exhibit. There will be hundreds of people there, and you can auction her off easily enough."

"Chick! What a crazy idea! It would never do!"

"Why not?"

"Well, first, Mrs. Meredith would be highly indignant at such a performance."

"Not she! You know very well, Patty, she's a climber; and she's most anxious to know you better, and count you as her friend. Oh, I know all this inside information, I do! So, if you do something a bit eccentric, perhaps, but pretty and effective it will give her tea a certain prestige, a unique interest that will tickle her to death."

Patty considered. "It might work," she said,

thinking hard; "but I'll have to go back and dress."

"So shall I. But the Belle of the Ball, here, is all right, isn't she?"

"Yes; or,—no,—I'll put on her very bestest frock, all lace and frills. Well, turn back home, then and come for us again at five. It's Milly's bed-time at six, but no matter, if we provide her a home and a career."

At five, then, Chick returned, and found a resplendent pair awaiting him. Patty wore one of her prettiest afternoon frocks, of Dolly Varden silk, and Milly was in gossamer linen and laces, hidden beneath her white cloth coat.

She was in effervescent spirits and babbled continuously in her merry little way.

At the house, the maid in the cloak-room stared hard at the baby, but said no word as she drew off the little coat sleeves.

Patty looked Milly over, critically, perked up her enormous pink hair-bow, and shook out her frills, then they went to the drawing-room, meeting Chick at the door.

"I feel a mad desire to giggle," he said, as he caught sight of Patty, and Milly toddling beside her.

"I feel a mad desire to run away," she returned. "Stand by me, Chick."

"*A la mort!*" he replied, and they entered the reception.

"How do you do, Mrs. Meredith?" said Patty, in her most dulcet tones. "I took the liberty of bringing a little friend of mine. Though she wasn't invited, I feel sure you can spare her a little bit of your welcome and hospitality."

Mrs. Meredith, a young woman of great dignity, looked at Milly in astonishment. As Patty had carefully taught her, the midget dropped a dainty courtesy, and smiled up in her hostess' face.

Remembering the great desirability of Patty's friendship, Mrs. Meredith retained her composure, and laughed. "You dear girl, how original you are! Who else would have thought of bringing a baby to my reception? Is she a relative of yours?"

"Not that," said Patty, smiling, "but a very dear friend."

And then Channing stepped up to greet Mrs. Meredith, and others quickly followed, so that our trio could drift away into the crowd of chatting, laughing people.

"What shall we do with Middy?" said Patty, anxiously. "The little thing will be smothered down there, among all those full skirts and floating sashes!"

For already the tiny mite was entangling her little fingers in the fringed ends of a lady's scarf.

"I'll take her," and Chick leaned down, and picking up Middy, seated her on his broad shoulder.

It made a bit of a sensation, for Channing's towering height made him always a conspicuous figure, and the laughing baby attracted every one's attention.

"Now's your chance!" he whispered suddenly. "Everybody is looking at us. Step up on this chair and auction her off! I *dare* you to!"

CHAPTER XIV

A GREAT SUCCESS

PATTY always declared afterward, that Chick hypnotised her, and that she *never* would have done it, had she been in her right mind.

But, on the spur of the moment, carried away with the spirit of the thing, knowing that it was then or never, and taunted by the "*dare*," Patty stepped up on the low chair, and said, "People Dear" before she realised what she was about. Then, like a flash, an acute realisation of what she had done, came over her, followed with lightning-like swiftness by the knowledge that she *must* go on. To go on was the only possible justification for having gone so far. So, go on, she did.

"Dear People, listen a minute. This is unconventional and all that, I know,—but just hark. Here is a little girl, a beautiful and well-born child, for somebody's adoption. Who wants her? Surely among all of you there is

[193]

some woman-heart who could love this dear baby enough to give her a home. Look at her! Is she not charming? And as bright and affectionate as she is pretty. Kiss your hand to the people, Milly."

Milly always obeyed the slightest wish of her beloved Patty, and with the most adorable smiles, and coy glances from her big, dark eyes, she blew kisses from her tiny finger-tips.

"Now love Mr. Chick," went on Patty, shaking in her shoes, lest this might try Channing's endurance beyond its limit.

But he was game, and when Milly's dimpled arms went round his neck and she laid her soft cheek against his hair, and crooned a few little love notes, the audience applauded with delight.

"You see," went on Patty, "this baby is homeless. I want to give her to a kind, wise and loving woman. No others need apply. I will say no more now, but any one who is interested may speak to me about it either here and now, or at my home. I will tell all particulars to any one who wants the baby, and will be the right mother for her."

Flushed with the excitement of the moment,

A Great Success

Patty made a deprecating little bow, and stepped down from the low chair.

There was a moment's silence, and then Milly's high, thin little voice piped out: "Me fink Patty booful!"

This disarmed criticism and everybody laughed, while a ripple of applause floated through the room. And then half a dozen of the ladies moved toward the end of the room where Patty and Milly were.

They were followed by others, for all wanted to see more closely the interesting mite, and the unusual circumstance roused curiosity even among those who had no thought of taking the child.

But it seemed several did want her, or at least wanted to investigate the matter.

Channing, by Patty's side, helped to answer questions. He was an invaluable aid, for his quick wit and pleasant personality made for a clear understanding of the case.

"Nonsense, Mrs. Fanning," he said to a gay young matron, "you don't want another olive branch! You've five at home, now!"

"I know it, but this is such a heavenly baby, and my youngest is eight. I'd love to have this

[195]

cherub, though I don't know what Mr. Fanning would say——"

"Now, you musn't be greedy," said Chick, smiling; " be content with your own little brood, and let somebody take Milly, who really needs an angel in the house."

Milly did not become frightened at the amount of curious attention she received, but serene and sweet, smiled happily at all, and cuddled close to Patty.

It was not difficult to discover who was really in earnest among the inquirers. Some were charmed by the baby's attractions, but had no thought of taking her to keep. Others looked at her wistfully, but for one reason or another were unable to adopt her. But there were three who were positive of their desire for the child, and each of the three was determined to have her.

" I offered first," argued Mrs. Chaffee, a haughty dame, whose dark eyes blazed angrily, as she noted Patty's indifference to her claim. " I wish to have the child, and I can give her every advantage."

" So can I," said Miss Penrose, a delightful middle-aged spinster, who wanted an heir to her fortune and a pet to lavish her affection

[196]

upon. " I want her very much. I can devote all my time and attention to her. She shall have the best of education and training, and my wealth shall all be hers."

Patty considered. Miss Penrose was of aristocratic family, and her prestige was undeniable. She would give all care and study to a most careful, correct bringing up of the baby, and Milly's future would be assured. But, and Patty did not herself realise at first why she objected to Miss Penrose, until it suddenly dawned on her that it was because the lady had no sense of humour! Patty was sure she would take the upbringing of Milly so seriously that the sunny baby would become a little automaton. This was instinctive on Patty's part, for she knew Miss Penrose only slightly, but the earnestness of the lady was very apparent.

Smilingly holding the question in abeyance, Patty listened to the plea of the third applicant. This was Mrs. Colton, a sad-faced, sweet-eyed young widow. Two years before, a motor accident had snatched from her her husband and baby girl, and had left her for a time hovering between life and death. Only of late, had she listened to her friends' urging to go among people once more, and this tea was almost her first appearance in society since her tragic affliction.

With tears in her eyes, she said to Patty: "I *must* have the baby. She is not unlike my little Gladys, and she would be to me a veritable Godsend. I have thought often of adopting a child, and this is the one I want. I love her already. Will you come to me, Milly?"

Milly eyed her. For a moment the two looked at each other intently. There was a breathless pause, and all who were near felt the dramatic intensity of the moment. Mrs. Colton smiled, and it may have been that Milly read in that smile all the pent-up mother-love and longing, for she dropped Patty's hand and walked slowly toward the lady,—her little arms outstretched. Reaching her, she threw her arms about her neck, exclaiming, "I fink you's booful!"

This phrase was her highest praise, and as Mrs. Colton's arms closed round the child, no one could doubt that these two hearts were forever united.

"I hope you *will* take her, Mrs. Colton," said Patty, earnestly; "you are made for each other."

"Indeed, I will take her, if I may. In fact, I cannot let her go!" and the tear-dimmed

[198]

eyes, full of affection, gazed at the little cherub.

"But *I* want her," declared Mrs. Chaffee. "I asked for her first, and I think it most unfair——"

"I'm not auctioning the baby, Mrs. Chaffee," said Patty, smiling at the determined lady; "it isn't a question of who asked first. Milly and Mrs. Colton are too perfectly suited to each other to let me even consider any other mother for the child. Please give up all thought of it, for I have made up my mind."

Miss Penrose was more acquiescent, and nonchalantly presumed she could get an equally pretty baby from an asylum. To which Patty heartily agreed.

It was arranged that Patty should take Milly home with her for a few days, till Mrs. Colton could prepare for her reception. Also, she promised to call in her lawyer and see about the legal processes of adoption in this most unusual case.

All unwitting of the plans for her destiny, Milly beamed impartially on everybody, and went with Patty to make adieux to the hostess.

"I do apologise," said Patty, smiling, "for this eccentric performance. But when you know me better, dear Mrs. Meredith, you will expect strange happenings when I'm about. All my friends know this."

The speech was a clever one, for Mrs. Meredith greatly desired to be classed among the friends of Patty Fairfield, the society belle.

"It was charming of you," she returned, "to choose my drawing-room for your pretty project. I trust you will always feel free to avail yourself of any opportunity I can offer."

Milly made her dear little curtesy; Channing murmured polite phrases, and they went away.

"Well!" said Chick, as they whirled along homeward, "we came, we saw, and you bet we conquered! How about it?"

"I should say we did!" and Patty's face glowed with satisfaction and happiness. "There's nobody I'd rather give Milly to than Mrs. Colton. She's a perfect dear, and her great sorrow has left her with an aching, hungry heart, that this little scrap of happiness can fill."

"You were a brick, Patty! I didn't think you'd dare do it."

"I couldn't have, if I'd stopped to think. But you dared me—and I never, could refuse a dare!"

"Then I claim some of the credit of the success of our scheme."

"All of it, Chick. I never should have dreamed of such an unheard of performance! What *will* Nan say?"

"Let's go in and see; may I come in?"

"Yes, do. I want you to back me up, if they jump on me."

But they didn't. Though Nan and Mr. Fairfield were utterly astounded at the story they heard, they had only praise for the result.

"The very one!" declared Nan. "Mrs. Colton is a lovely woman, and her wealth and education and refined tastes will insure Milly exactly the right kind of a home for life. Oh, Patty, it's fine! But what *did* Mrs. Meredith think?"

"Oh," said Patty, airily, "as it was the illustrious Me, she was overjoyed to have her house turned into an auction room! She would have been equally delighted if I'd made a bear garden of it."

"You conceited little rascal," said her father, shocked at this self-esteem.

"No, it wasn't *my* idea. You all know *my* overweening modesty. But Chick, here, said that the parvenu element in the lady's soul would be kindly disposed toward,—well, let us say, toward the daughter of Frederick Fairfield."

This turning of the tables made them all laugh, but Channing said, " It's quite true. I know the Meredith type, and I was sure that to be made conspicuous by an acknowledged social power, like our Patty, would be unction to her soul."

" Well, it was a crazy piece of business," said Mr. Fairfield, " but as it turned out so admirably, we can't complain. It is right down splendid, to get the little one taken by such a fine woman as Mrs. Colton. I'm sure it will be a most successful arrangement. And we owe you a vote of thanks, Channing, for bringing it about."

" Oh, I'm only accessory before the fact. Patty did it. I wish you could have seen her when she mounted that chair! It was as good as a play. Her do-or-die expression, concealed beneath a society smile, was a whole show! "

" I don't care, I accomplished my purpose," and Patty beamed with satisfaction; " but it was mostly because Chick dared me! "

" Let us hope I'll always be present at any crisis in your life to dare you! " said Chan-

[202]

ning. "It's an easy way to achieve great results."

When Patty's friends heard of her episode, they bombarded her with telephone messages and notes and calls concerning it. Some chaffed her and others praised, but all were agog over the matter. Even Mrs. Van Reypen telephoned to know if the report she had heard were true.

"What did you hear?" asked Patty.

"That you went to a tea and auctioned off a baby."

"No, that isn't quite the true version of what happened. Now, I'll tell you."

"No, don't. I can't bear to talk over the telephone. Come and see me, and bring that child along. I want to see it."

Mrs. Van Reypen's wish was usually looked upon as a command, and the next afternoon Patty started off with Milly to call on her elderly friend.

"What a baby! Oh, *what* a baby!" was the greeting the child received, for Mrs. Van Reypen was most enthusiastic. "Why didn't you keep her yourself? How can you let her go? I never saw such a lovely baby!"

"She is," agreed Patty, smiling, as Milly curt-sied to Mrs. Van Reypen over and over again. "But I couldn't keep her. I don't want the care and responsibility of a kiddy. Would you have liked to take her?"

"I believe I would, if you had offered me the chance. But no, I am too old to train a baby now. Do you know, though, Patty, the care of orphan children has always appealed to me as one of the best of philanthropies. I sometimes think even yet I will start a home for such little waifs. I mean a real homelike sort of a place,—not the institution usually founded for such a purpose."

"It would be a splendid thing, Lady Van. Go ahead, and do it. I will help you, if I can."

"Would you, Patty? Would you give of your time and interest to help establish the thing, and be one of the workers for it?"

"Yes, I would. I don't want the entire re-sponsibility of little Milly, but I am glad I've found a good home for her. And if there are other similar little unfortunates, and of course there are, I'd be more than willing to help you in a project to make them happy and cared for."

"Well, I'll remember that, and I think I'll set

[204]

about planning for it. I'm getting older all the time, and what I do, ought to be begun soon. Patty, you are very dear to me,—you know that?"

"It's kind of you to say so, Lady Van, and I do appreciate and greatly value your affection for me. I wish I could do something to show my love in return, and if you decide to go into this scheme of yours, call on me for any help I can give."

"Thank you, dear. But, Patty, there is another way in which you could greatly please me, —if you—but I think you know."

Patty did know what was coming, but she affected ignorance. "'Most any way, Lady Van, I'm glad to please you, but I think this Orfling Home plan the most feasible and practicable. When shall us begin?"

"But I'm not thinking of that just now. Patty, you dear girl,—don't you—*can't* you bring yourself to care for Philip?"

"Oh, I do care for Phil. I care for him a lot. We're the greatest chums. He'll help us with the new scheme, won't he?"

"But I mean to care for him, especially. The way he cares for you."

"Now, dear Lady Van, let's not discuss that

today. I'm so busy getting this matter of Milly fixed up, I can't turn to other topics. Don't you think it would be nice for me to get a sort of wardrobe together for her, before she goes to Mrs. Colton's?"

"No. I think it would be ridiculous! Mrs. Colton has plenty of means, and she has taste and knows what is right and proper for the child far better than you do. Give the baby a parting gift if you like—I'll give her one myself. I'll give her a silver porringer. She's 'most too big for a porringer, but she can keep it for an heirloom. The one I mean to give her is an old Dutch one of real value. But, Patty, as to Philip."

"Not now, please, Lady Van, dear," and Patty put her fingers to her ears.

"Well, some other time, then. But, Patty, if you could learn to care for my boy, I'd—I'd make you my heir."

"Oh, fie, fie, Lady Van! You're trying to buy my young affections? Now, you mustn't do that. And, too, don't you know that the best way to make me dislike Phil is to continually urge him upon me."

Mrs. Van Reypen looked a little taken aback at this, and immediately dropped the subject,

[206]

for which Patty was devoutly thankful. She did like Philip, but she did not want his aunt arranging affairs for her, for Patty was an independent nature, and especially so where her plans for her own future were concerned.

So she gladly turned the conversation back to the matter of the Children's Home, and soon realised that Mrs. Van Reypen was greatly in earnest about it, and that it might soon become a reality.

CHAPTER XV

PATTY'S FUTURE

ONE day Patty was at a matinée with some of the girls, when Mrs. Van Reypen called at the Fairfield home. It being Saturday afternoon, Mr. Fairfield was at home, and the visitor asked to see him as well as his wife.

After greetings were exchanged, the straightforward old lady went at once to her subject.

"I've come to see you about Patty," she began, "and if you choose to tell me I'm a meddlesome old woman and concerning myself with what is none of my business, you will be quite within your rights."

"I doubt we shall do that, Mrs. Van Reypen," said Fred Fairfield, pleasantly. "What is it about Patty?"

"Only this. To put it in plain words, I want her to marry my nephew Philip."

"I should make no objections to that. Indeed, I should be glad and proud to have my daughter become the wife of your nephew. He is a fine man. I feel that I know him well and there is no one to whom I would rather entrust Patty's happiness."

"Thank you, Mr. Fairfield. Phil *is* a good boy, and I have yet to learn a mean or ignoble thing about him. What is your opinion, Mrs. Fairfield?"

"I quite agree with my husband," returned Nan. "Philip has always been one of my favourites among Patty's friends, and I, too, should hear of their engagement with pleasure. But, Mrs. Van Reypen, we cannot answer for Patty herself. She is, as you perhaps know, a self-willed young person, and not to be driven or even advised, against her will."

"But that's just it. Patty doesn't know her own will. She takes for granted all the attentions and favours of the young men, and, goodness knows she gets enough of them, but it never seems to occur to her that it's time she thought about making a choice of one in particular."

"Oh, come, now, Mrs. Van Reypen, Patty is not yet climbing up on the traditional shelf."

"I know that, Mr. Fairfield, but the point is, that she is heart-whole and fancy-free, and while she is, I desire to influence her mind toward Philip. Yes, just that. It is not wrong; on the contrary, it is a wise thing to do. In France the girls' betrothals are always arranged by their elders. In England they frequently are. And there is no reason the plan shouldn't obtain in our country. We all have Patty's best interests at heart, and if we can help this thing along,—without letting the child know it, of course,—it is our duty as well as our pleasure to do it."

"But how, Mrs. Van Reypen?" asked Nan. "Patty would quickly resent any interference or dictation in her affairs; and, too, any hint that we were helping Philip's cause along, would, I assure you, react disastrously to our effort."

"Oh, certainly, if she *knew* it," and Mrs. Van Reypen spoke impatiently; "but she needn't know it."

"How, then, shall it be done?"

"In lots of ways. Let us throw them together whenever possible. See to it that she accepts his invitations here and there. Place them next each other at dinners; in a word, make it clear to the other members of their circle, that they are definitely *for* each other, and it will shortly be recognized and accepted as a fact. I will give opera parties and dinner parties, and I will see to it, that they are conspicuously paired as partners."

"That sounds plausible, Mrs. Van Reypen," and Nan shook her head; "but it is not so easy. You, of course, see them together often, but Patty goes to many parties where Philip is not invited, or if he *is* there, where she is escorted by some one else."

"That's just it!" and the old lady's tone was vibrant with enthusiasm; "we must see to it that she is invited everywhere first by Philip, and then she can't accept these other invitations."

Nan smiled at the thought of thus ordering headstrong Patty's engagement calendar, but she only said, "I'm sure if you can accomplish this, I shall be but too glad. For I, too, want to see Patty happily married. I am in no haste for the event to occur, but I would like to rest assured that her choice will be a wise one, and one that will mean her lifelong happiness."

"All that would be insured by her betrothal to Philip," and Philip's aunt looked complacent. "And I am sure the dear girl would be willing to say yes to him, if she were convinced that it was time for her to make a choice. Will you not, both of you, do all you can to bring this about?"

"With pleasure," said Mr. Fairfield, "but, as my wife says, it is not easy to force or coerce my daughter."

"Oh, not force or coerce! Have you people no idea of diplomacy? Of strategy, even, if necessary?"

"Just how may diplomacy be directly employed?"

"Principally, perhaps, by inducing propinquity. The more they are together, the more they will care for one another. Though to be sure, Philip is deeply in love with Patty, now. He has, I am sure, asked her to marry him already."

"Then if he has, and she has refused him," said Nan, "what more can we do?"

"Refused him? Nothing of the sort! She hasn't accepted him, of course, or we would know of it; but you know how girls, nowadays, play fast and loose with a man, if they are sure of his devotion. Indeed, if Philip could be persuaded to slight Patty a little, now and then, it would soon pique her into an acceptance. But he will never do that,—I know him too well.

Philip is a dear boy, but a straightforward nature, with no thought of trifling or deception. No, we must devote our efforts toward Patty's attitude, not Philip's. He is all right as he is. If Patty will consent to marry my nephew, I am considering making her my heiress."

"Mrs. Van Reypen!" Fred Fairfield exclaimed in indignation, " I beg you will not use any such argument or bribe in connection with my daughter's name!"

"Hoity-toity, now! Don't get excited. 'Tis no bribe. 'Tis but the fact; if so be that Patty will become my niece, I shall divide my wealth equally between her and my nephew. She shall have half in her own right. If she will not, half is still Philip's and the other half will go to a charity. I don't want to give it all to Philip. He is already a rich man, and I don't approve of too big fortunes for young men."

"Never mind about the money part of it," said Nan. " I am quite willing to espouse Mrs. Van Reypen's cause, irrespective of her will. And, too, if Patty does marry Philip, it is quite right and proper that she should inherit this wealth. If not, there is no question of her having it. So the fortune element settles itself. But what I can't see is how we're going about this thing. I'm somewhat practical, Mrs. Van Reypen, and I confess I can see no practical way to bring these two hearts to beat as one. If you can instruct me, I shall be glad to obey orders."

Nan looked very pretty and sweet as she spoke in earnest on the subject. She meant just what she said. She would be very glad to have Patty marry Philip, very glad to do anything she could to help bring it about, but for the life of her she couldn't see anything to do.

"Well," Mrs. Van Reypen defended her stand, "when I took them on that motor trip together with me, that was a step in the right direction. They were thrown so much in one another's company, that it became inevitable to them to be together. I always thought if that Mr. Farnsworth hadn't joined us up at Lake Sunapee, the matter would have been settled then and there."

"You think Mr. Farnsworth interfered?" asked Nan.

"I'm not sure. Do you think Patty cares for him?"

"No, I think not," said Fred Fairfield. "They seem to have little tiffs when they're together, and I doubt they are very congenial."

Patty's Future

"I used to like Bill Farnsworth," said Nan, "but since I learned that he tried to bring about Patty's going on the stage, I've not cared so much for him. You see, he's a Westerner, and he has different ideas from ours. Imagine Patty on the stage! And it was unpardonable in him to put the idea in her head."

"Did he do that?"

"Yes, Philip said he heard that Mr. Farnsworth took Patty over to the hotel where that actress was staying, to talk the matter over. And he says that Patty herself said that Bill said she was good-looking enough to go on the stage! Fancy!"

"It's an outrage! That whole stage business makes my blood boil!" and Mrs. Van Reypen's very bonnet strings shook in righteous indignation. "That's what you get for letting her associate with a man like that."

"Oh, come now," said Mr. Fairfield, "Farnsworth is a good sort. I think he's very much of a man."

"A fine type of a man to try to get a nice girl like Patty to become a common actress!" The aristocratic visitor's face expressed the deepest scorn of the theatrical profession as a whole. "But she's all over that, isn't she?"

"Yes, thank goodness!" answered Nan. "Well, all I can see to do, is, to incline Patty toward Philip in any subtle way we can. Praise him to her, judiciously, not too much. Compare him favourably with other men, especially Mr. Farnsworth, for I'm not sure that Patty doesn't like him quite a little. Then let Philip come here often and we will make him very welcome, and the rest I think he will have to accomplish himself."

"You have expressed it very well, Mrs. Fairfield," and the visitor rose to go. "And I'm sure other ways and means will suggest themselves to you as time goes on. If you would sometimes ask him to dinner quite *en famille,* I will do the same by Patty. Such things,—letting them be alone together of an evening now and then,—will do wonders."

And so the plans were made, and the schemers, who were all actuated by an honest desire for Patty's happiness, began to watch for opportunities.

As Mrs. Van Reypen had surmised, in her wise, canny mind, there were ways, unobtrusive and delicate, by which the two young people could be thrown together more frequently and none of these was neglected. Nothing insistent or noticeable was ever attempted, but after a time, Patty found herself relying on Philip's advice and judgment, and unconsciously referring questions to him for settlement.

Mrs. Van Reypen and the elder Fairfields noted this approvingly, and the whole circle of young people came gradually to look on Philip as Patty's special property.

Van Reypen was by no means averse to this, and he adopted an attitude of ownership, which, as it became definite, was quickly resented by Patty.

"Look here, Phil," she said one day; "you needn't act as if I belonged to you. Don't decide things for me without my consent."

"Forgive me, Patty. I've no wish to offend. But you will belong to me some day, and I suppose I'm too impatient for the day to come."

"How do you know I will?"

"It's written in the stars. We were made for each other. You'll wake up to the fact some day, perhaps soon."

"I ha'e me doots," said Patty, in roguish mood, and her light laughter checked the more serious words that rose to Philip's lips. He was content to bide his time.

[217]

One day he telephoned to Patty that Mrs. Van Reypen was not well and begged she would come over.

" Is she ill? " asked Patty in surprise, for the hale old lady was a valetudinarian.

" Not quite that, but she has a cold, and she wants cheering up."

So Patty ordered the car and went right over. She found that Mrs. Van Reypen did, indeed, have a cold, and a severe one. Patty was alarmed and insisted on calling the doctor, who pronounced it a case of grip, and ordered the patient to bed.

Patty remained over night, for Mrs. Van Reypen was feverish and too nervous and worried about herself to be left to the care of servants. Late in the evening, however, she became quieter, and begged Patty to leave her to herself for a time, and go downstairs and sit with Philip and cheer up the poor boy.

So, having made the sick lady as comfortable as she could, Patty ran downstairs for a while.

She was garbed in a boudoir robe of Mrs. Van Reypen's. She had discarded her street gown as being out of place in the sick room, and had rummaged in her hostess' wardrobe until she selected one of the many house gowns and negligées that hung there.

It was utterly inappropriate for the girl, being made of purple silk, with a wide berthé of Duchess lace. But it made Patty look very quaint and sweet,—like a maid of olden time. She had twisted her curls up high, and added a large carved ivory comb, from the dressing table.

"The Puritan Maiden, Priscilla," she had said, laughingly as she pirouetted before her hostess.

"A very fetching garb," remarked the old lady. "You may have it to keep. You can use it in your amateur theatricals, or such dressings up, and the berthé is of valuable old lace."

Patty thanked her kind friend, but to tell the truth, she was so accustomed to receiving gifts from Mrs. Van Reypen that one more was but as a drop in the bucket.

So, on being dismissed from the sick room, Patty ran lightly downstairs, and into the library. Only a shaded table light was turned on, and in the glow of the firelight Philip sat, in an easy chair, smoking. When he heard Patty enter, he threw his cigar in the fire, and holding out his arm, he drew her down to the broad tufted arm of the great chair he sat in.

"How goes it upstairs?" he asked, casually.

"Not very well," said Patty, soberly. "I don't want to be a 'calamity howler,' but I think Lady Van is more ill than she knows. This grip is a treacherous thing, and liable to take sudden turns for the worse. And, too, she is not as young as she once was, and so, Philip, I want you to take all precautions. I will look after her tonight, but tomorrow you must get a nurse."

"Of course I will. Send for one now, if you say so."

"No, I can manage for tonight. She is resting quietly now. She is bright and cheery, you understand, but she is weak, and the disease has a strong hold on her."

"Patty, what a dear girl you are!" Philip spoke in a fine, honest, manly way, and Patty thrilled at his so sincere praise. "You are one in a thousand! Indeed, I'm sure there never was another like you."

"Go 'way wid yer blarney," laughed Patty, a least bit embarrassed because she knew it was not mere blarney.

"It's the truth, dear, and you know it. Oh,

Patty, wouldn't it be nice if you lived here all the time?"

"So I could take care of Lady Van?" and her light laugh rang out.

"Yes, and so you could take care of me. I need taking care of,—that is, I need you to take care of me."

"Why, Philip, you're the most capable person I know. You can take care of yourself."

"Well, then, I wish you lived here so I could take care of you. Would you like that, you little Colonial Dame?"

"I'm pretty independent. I'm not sure I'd take kindly to being taken care of."

"You would like the way *I'd* take care of you, I promise you that!"

"Why, how would it be?"

Patty knew she was playing with fire. She knew that unless she meant to encourage Philip Van Reypen, she ought not to lead him on in this way. But Patty was very feminine, and the temptation to know just what he meant was very strong.

"Well," Philip laid his warm hand gently on hers, "in the first place, you should never know a care or a trouble that I could bear for you."

"H'm," said Patty, "that's comforting, but not so very entertaining."

"You little witch! Do you want entertainment? Well, then, I'd make it my life work to invent new entertainments for you every day. How's that?"

"That's better," and naughty Patty showed animated delight at the prospect. "What would the entertainments be like?"

"That's telling. They'd be surprises, and I can't divulge their secrets till you do come to live here?"

"I did live here once," said Patty, smiling at the recollection. "As Lady Van's companion."

"And now won't you come and live here as my companion?"

"Oh, are you getting old enough to need a companion?"

"I sure am! I'm twenty-six, and that's the very exact age when a man wants a companion, or, at any rate, this man does. Will you, Patty Precious?"

"I dunno. Tell me more about these entertainments."

"Well, they should comprise all the best ones that are to be found on the face of the earth.

And when you tired of them, I would make up new ones."

" Parties ? "

" Yes, parties of every sort. Dances, theatre parties, motor parties, dinner parties,——"

" And little twosy parties,—just you and me all alone ? "

" Patty! you witch! do you want to drive me crazy? Now, just for that, you've got to say yes, and live here with me, and have all the little twosy parties you want ! "

" But, Philip, *I* proposed them, you didn't! " and Patty pouted until her scarlet lips looked like a cleft cherry.

" Because I didn't dare. Do you suppose I let myself think that you would care for such? "

" Well, I don't know as I do. I've never tried them! " And Patty ran out of the room.

CHAPTER XVI

THE PROMISE

ON returning to Mrs. Van Reypen's room, Patty found that lady sleeping quietly, so she herself went to bed on a couch in the dressing-room adjoining. Next morning, the patient was weak and ill, and when the doctor arrived he sent at once for two nurses. Patty went home, feeling sad, for she feared her kind old friend might not survive this illness.

But Nan cheered her up, saying that while grip was sometimes a serious matter, more often, it was light and of short duration.

"But it is contagious," Nan went on, "and I don't want you to catch it, Patty. Don't go over there again, until Mrs. Van Reypen gets better."

Patty agreed to this, but a few days later, there came such an imperative summons from Mrs. Van Reypen that Patty felt she must respond to the call.

The Promise

"Well, don't go very near her," begged Nan, as Patty started. "You are susceptible to colds, and if you get grip, it will wear you out."

Reaching the house, Patty was shocked at the appearance of Mrs. Van Reypen. She was emaciated and her face had a waxen pallor. But her dark eyes were feverishly bright, and she greeted Patty with an eager smile. Then she sent the nurse from the room, with peremptory orders not to return until called.

"Patty, I want to talk to you," the old lady began.

"All right, Lady Van," said Patty, lightly, "but you musn't talk much. If it's an important subject, you'd better wait till you are stronger."

"I shall never be stronger, my dear. This is my last illness,——"

"Oh, now, don't talk like that. Grip always makes its patients discouraged, but you are too sensible to be fooled by it. Brace up, and resolve to get well, and then you will get well."

Patty was arguing against her own convictions, for she saw the ravages the disease had made, and she feared the worst. But she did all she could to cheer and encourage.

"It's useless for you to talk like that," the invalid went on, " for I know what I know. Now listen to me. I am going to die. I know it, and I am not afraid. I am seventy years old, I have have had a happy life, and if my time has come, I am willing to die. Life is sweet, but we must all die, and it is only a coward who fears death. I am going to leave you a fortune, Patty. I have made my will and in it, I bequeath you a hundred thousand dollars."

"Oh, Lady Van," Patty gasped, " don't, *don't* leave me all that money! I should be overcome with the responsibility of it."

"Nonsense! But listen to the plan. I want you to have half of it absolutely for yourself, and the other half, use to build a Children's Home. I know you will enjoy doing this, and I trust you to do it well. Thus, you see, your own share of the money is, in a way, payment for your work and responsibility of the Home. You may build, rent, or buy a house for the purpose. Your father and Philip will help you as to the business matters. But the furnishing and house planning will be your work. Will you do this?"

"I'd love to do it!" and Patty's eyes shone at the idea. "If I am capable."

"Of course you're capable. Not a big Home, you understand, but as large as the money will properly pay for. Then, have it bright and pretty, and if it only accommodates a dozen children, I don't care. I know this is your favourite form of philanthropy and it is also mine. I wish we could have done it together, but it is too late for that now. But Philip will help you, and if more money is necessary, he will give it to you, from his own inheritance. Phil is a rich man, but I shall leave him all my fortune except what I give you. So don't hesitate to ask him if you need more funds."

"All right, but I shall put your whole bequest into the scheme. I don't want to be paid for doing what will be a great pleasure."

"Don't be a little simpleton! You will take your own half for your individual use, and not a cent of it is to go toward the Home. There is money enough for that. And it isn't payment. I give it to you, because I am really very fond of you. You have made sunshine in my life ever since I first found you, and I am glad to give you a small fortune. When you marry, as you will some day, you will find it very nice to be able to buy what you want for your trousseau. You can buy worth-while jewels with it, or, if you prefer, put it out at interest and have a stated income. But accept it you must, or I shall think you don't love me at all."

"Oh, yes, I do. Dear Lady Van, you know I do."

"Then don't upset my last hours by refusing what I offer."

Patty almost laughed at the snappish tone, so incongruous in one who was making a splendid gift. But Mrs. Van Reypen was getting more and more excited. A red spot burned in either cheek, and her eyes blazed as she gesticulated from her pillows.

"And there's another thing, Patty Fairfield, that you are to do for me. You are to marry my boy, Philip."

"Well," and Patty laughed lightly, "we won't discuss that now."

"But we will discuss it now. I want your promise. Do you suppose I got you over here just to tell you about my will? No. I want you to promise me that you will grant me this happiness before I die. Philip loves you deeply. He wants you for his wife and he has told you so. Where could you find a better man? A more honourable, a kinder, a more generous and loving heart? And he worships you. He would always be gentle and tender with you. He is of fine old stock, there is no better family tree in the country than the Van Reypens. Now, will you give me your promise?"

"Oh, Lady Van, I can't promise offhand, like this. You must let me think it over."

"You've had time enough for that. Tell me, —you care for Philip, don't you?"

"Yes, indeed I care for him a great deal,—as a friend. But I don't think I love him as I ought to—as I want to love the man I marry."

"Fiddlesticks! You don't know your own mind, that's all. You're a foolish, sentimental child. Now, look here, you marry Philip soon, —and you'll find out that you do love him. Why, who could help it? He's such a splendid fellow. He would make you as happy as the day is long. Patty, he's a man of a thousand. He hasn't a bad trait or an unworthy thought in his mind. You don't know how really fine he is. And he adores you so,—he would give you every wish of your heart."

"I know he would. He has told me so. But I can't feel sure that I care for him in the right way. And I can't promise——"

"You mean you won't! You are willing to

trifle with Philip's affections and lead him on and lure him with false hopes and then——"

"Stop, stop! That's not fair! I never led him on! We have been good friends for years, but I never even imagined his wanting to marry me until he told me so last summer."

"Last summer! And you haven't given him a definite answer yet! You keep him on tenter-hooks without the least consideration or care as to his feelings. If he were not such a patient man, he would have given up all idea of wanting you. Do you know what you are, Patty Fairfield? You're a little flirt, that's what you are! You ought to be ashamed of yourself! How many other men have you on a string? Several, I dare say."

"Lady Van, you have no right to talk to me like this? If you were not ill, I'd be very angry with you. But as you are, I ascribe your harsh speeches to the illness that is racking you. Now, let us drop the subject and talk of something pleasanter."

"We'll do nothing of the sort! I sent for you to get your promise, and I'm going to get it!" Mrs. Van Reypen sat upright in her bed, and shook her clenched hand at Patty. "You little fool!" she cried, "any girl in her senses would be only too glad to get such a man as my nephew! You are honoured by his wanting you. I am very fond of you myself,—you are so pretty and sunny-faced. But if you refuse me this wish of my heart, I shall cease to love you. I won't leave you that money, I——"

The old lady's voice rose nearly to a shriek, and she glared at Patty with a fairly malevolent gaze.

That last speech was too much for Patty.

"I don't want your money," she said, rising to go. "I cannot stay and listen to such unjust remarks as you have been making. I'm sorry, but I can't give you the promise you ask, and as I can't please you I think I'd better go."

"Sit down," begged Mrs. Van Reypen, and now her anger was gone, and her tones were wheedlesome. "Forgive me, dear, I have no right to force your will. But please, Patty Girl, think it over, here and now. You can easily learn to love Phil,—you're not in love with anybody else, are you?"

"No," replied Patty.

"Then, as I say, you can easily learn to love him, he is such a dear. And he would treat you like a princess. He would shower you with gifts and pleasures. You could live in this house, or he would buy you or build you whatever home you fancied. Then, together, you could carry out my project for the Children's Home. Your life would be a heaven on earth. Don't you think so, Patty,—dear Patty?"

When Lady Van chose she could be very sweet and ingratiating. And she seemed to hypnotize Patty. The girl looked at her with a hesitating expression.

"Say yes," pleaded the old lady. "Please, Patty, say yes. You'll never regret it, and you will be happy all your life. And you will have the satisfaction of knowing that you eased the last hours of a dying woman and sent her out of the world happy and contented to go. For I am dying, Patty. You do not know all of my ills. I may live a few days, but not longer. The doctor knows and so do the nurses. I haven't told Philip, for I hate to cause him pain. But if I can tell him of your promise to marry him, it will mitigate his grief at saying farewell to me. Now you will say yes, won't you, my dear little Patty Girl?"

"But——"

"No buts now. You couldn't have the heart to refuse the dying request of one who has always loved you like a daughter. I would gladly

[232]

have adopted you, Patty, had your people been willing to spare you. I went to see your parents not long ago. Your father said there is no man in the world he would rather see you marry than Philip. And Mrs. Nan said the same. Why do you fight against it so? Is it merely shyness? Just maidenly reserve? If that's it, I understand and appreciate. But waive all that, for my time is short. You needn't marry him at once if you don't wish, but promise me that he shall be your choice. That he will be the man you will some day wed and make happy. Won't you promise, Patty?"

"I—can't——"

"Yes, you can!" Mrs. Van Reypen leaned out of her bed, and grasped Patty's arm in a vise-like clutch. "You can and you shall! Now,—at once! Promise!"

The black eyes of the old lady bored into Patty's own. Her firm, hard mouth was set in a straight line. And with both hands she gripped Patty's arms and shook her slightly. "Promise, or I shall die on the spot!"

"I promise," said Patty, faintly, urged on by the older woman's force of intensity of will.

Mrs. Van Reypen fell back exhausted. She seemed unconscious, but whether in a faint, or stunned by sudden reaction, Patty did not know.

She flew to the door and called the nurse.

"Goodness! What happened?" inquired Miss French. "Has she had any sort of mental shock?"

"She has given me one," returned Patty, but the nurse was busy administering restoratives, and paid no heed.

Patty went slowly downstairs and out into the street. She walked home in a daze. What had she done? For to Patty a promise was a sacred thing and not to be broken. She hoped Mrs. Van Reypen would get better and she would go and ask to be released from a promise that was fairly wrung from her. She was undecided whether to tell Nan about it or not, but concluded to wait a day or two first. And then, she thought to herself, why wasn't she prepared to fulfill the promise? Why didn't she want to marry Phil, big, kind-hearted Phil, who loved her so deeply? At times it almost seemed as if she did want to marry him, and then again, she wasn't sure.

"I'll sleep over it," she thought, "and by tomorrow I'll know my own mind better. I must be a very wobbly-brained thing, anyhow. Why

The Promise

don't I know what I want? But I suppose every girl feels like this when she tries to make up her mind. Philip is a dear, that's certain. Maybe I'm worrying too much over it. Well, I'll see by tomorrow."

But the next day and the next, Patty was equally uncertain as to whether she was glad or sorry that she had made that promise.

And after another day or two she went down herself with the grip.

"I told you you'd catch it from Mrs. Van Reypen," scolded Nan. "You had no business to go there and expose yourself."

"But I had to go when she sent for me," said Patty.

"What did she want of you? you never told me."

"Well, for one thing, she thinks she's going to die, and she wants to leave me a hundred thousand dollars in her will."

"A hundred thousand! Patty, you must be crazy."

"Well, it isn't all for me, only half." And then Patty told about the plan for the Children's Home, but she said nothing about the promise she had given.

Nan was greatly excited over the bequest.

[235]

"But," she said, "I don't believe Mrs. Van is going to die. She's better today. I just telephoned."

"I hope she won't die," said Patty fervently. "I don't want her money, and if she gets well she can run that Home project herself, and I'll willingly help. Oh, Nan, I do feel horrid."

Grip has the reputation of making people feel horrid. The doctor came and sent Patty to bed, and for several days she had a high fever, which was aggravated by her mental worry over the promise she had made to Mrs. Van Reypen.

CHAPTER XVII

THE CRISIS

AND then the day came when the doctor said Patty had pneumonia. Rooms were darkened; nurses went around silently; Nan wandered about, unable to concentrate her mind on anything and Mr. Fairfield spent much of his time at home.

The telephone was continually ringing, as one friend after another asked how Patty was, and the rooms downstairs were filled with the gifts of flowers that the patient might not even see.

"What word, Doctor?" asked Mona Galbraith, as the physician came downstairs, one morning. The girls came and went as they chose. Always some one or more of them were sitting in the library or living-room, anxiously awaiting news.

"I think I can say she's holding her own," replied the doctor, guardedly; "if she had a stronger constitution, I should feel decidedly hopeful. But she is a frail little body, and we must be very, very careful."

[237]

He hurried away, and Mona turned back to where Elise sat.

"I know she'll die," wailed Elise. "I just *know* Patty will die. Oh, it seems *such* a shame! I can't *bear* it!" and she broke down in a tumult of sobbing.

"Don't, Elise," begged Mona. "Why not hope for the best? Patty isn't strong,—but she's a healthy little piece, and that doctor is a calamity howler, anyway. Everybody says so."

"I know it, but somehow I have a presentiment Patty never will get well."

"Presentiments are silly things! They don't mean a thing! I'd rather have hope than all the presentiments in the world. Here comes Roger."

Knowing his sister and his fiancée were there, Roger came in. They told him what the doctor had said.

"Brace up, girls," he said, cheeringly. "The game's never out till it's played out. I believe our spunky little Patty will outwit the old pneumonia and get the better of it. She always comes out top of the heap somehow. And her holding on so long is a good sign. Don't you want to go home now, Mona? You look all tired out."

The Crisis

"Yes, do go, Mona," said Elise, kindly. "But it isn't tiredness, Roger, it's anxiety. Go on, you two, I'll stay a while longer."

The pair went, and Elise sat alone in the library.

Presently, through the stilled house, she heard Patty's voice ring out, high and shrill.

"I don't *want* it!" Patty cried; "I don't *want* the fortune! And I don't want to marry *anybody!* Why do they make me *promise* to marry everybody in the whole world?"

The voice was that of delirium. Though not really delirious, Patty's mind was flighty, and the sentences that followed were disjointed and incoherent. But they all referred to a fortune or to a marriage.

"What can she mean?" sobbed Nan, who, with her husband, sat in an adjoining room.

"Never mind, dear, it's her feverish, disordered imagination talking. If she were herself, she wouldn't know what those words meant. Perhaps it is better that her mind wanders. Some say that's a good sign. Keep up hope, Nan, darling, if only for my sake."

"Yes, Fred. And we have cause for hope. Doctor is by no means discouraged, and if we can tide over another twenty-four hours——"

"Yes—if we can——"

"We will! Something tells me Patty will get well. The clear look in her eyes this morning——"

"Were they clear, Nan? Did they seem so to you?"

"Yes, dear, they did. And the nurse said that meant a lot."

"But the specialist doctor—he said Patty is so frail——"

"So she is, and always has been. But that's in her favour. It's often the strong, robust people that go off quickest with pneumonia. Patty has a wiry, nervous strength that is a help to her now."

"You're such a comfort, Nan. But I don't want Patty to die."

"Nor I, Fred. She is nearly as dear to me as to you. You know that, I'm sure. And Patty is a born fighter. She's like you in that. I know she'll battle with that disease and conquer it,—I *know* she will!"

"Please God you're right, dearest. Let us hope it with all our hearts."

Alone, Patty fought her life and death battle. Doctors, nurses, friends, all did what they could, but alone she grappled with the angel of death. All unconsciously, too, but with an involuntary struggle for life against the grim foe that held her. Now and again her voice cried out in delirium or murmured in a babbling monotone.

Now racked with fever, now shivering with a chill, the tortured little body shook convulsively or lay in a death-like stupor.

Once, when Kit Cameron was downstairs, they heard Patty shriek out about the fortune.

"Oh," said Kit, awestruck; "can she mean that fortune-telling business we had? Don't you remember I told her she'd inherit a fortune. Of course, I was only joking. Fortune-tellers always predict a legacy. I hope *that* hasn't worried her."

"No," said Nan, shaking her head, "it isn't that. She's been worrying about that fortune ever since she's been flighty. I know what she means. Never mind it."

Glad that it was not an unfortunate result of his practical joke, Kit dropped the subject.

"I want her to get well so terribly," he went on. "I just *can't* have it otherwise. I've always cherished a sort of forlorn hope that I could win her yet. Do you think I've a chance, Mrs. Nan?"

"When we get her well again, we'll see," and Nan tried to speak cheerfully. "But it's awfully nice of you boys to come round so often. You cheer us up a good deal. Mr. Fairfield is not very hopeful. You see Patty's mother died so young, and Patty is very like her, delicate, fragile, though almost never really ill. And here comes another of my boys."

Nan always called Patty's friends her boys; and they all liked the pleasant, lively young matron, and affectionately called her Mrs. Nan.

This time it was Chick Channing, and he came to inquire after Patty, and also to bring the sad news that Mrs. Van Reypen was dead.

Though not entirely unexpected, for the old lady had been very ill, it was a shock, and cast a deeper gloom over the household.

"I'm so sorry for Philip," said Nan. "He was devoted to his aunt, and she idolised him. Of late, he practically made his home with her."

"I suppose he is her heir," observed Channing.

"I suppose so," returned Nan, listlessly. And then she suddenly remembered what Patty had said about Mrs. Van's bequest to her. But she decided to make no mention of it at present.

"She was a wealthy old lady," said Cameron.

The Crisis

"Van Reypen will be well fixed. He's a good all-round man, I like him."

"I don't know him well," said Chick, "I met him a few times. A thorough aristocrat, I should say."

"All of that. They're among the oldest of the Knickerbockers. But nothing of the snob about him. A right down good fellow and a loyal friend. Well, I must go. Command me, Mrs. Nan, if I can do the least thing for our Patty Girl. Keep up a good heart, and——"

Kit's voice choked, and he went off without further words.

Channing soon followed, but all day the young people kept calling or telephoning, for Patty had hosts of friends and they all loved her.

Nan went to her room to write a note of sympathy to Philip. Her own heart full of sorrow and anxiety, she felt deeply for the young man whose home death had invaded, and her kindred trouble helped her to choose the right words of comfort and cheer.

The day of Mrs. Van Reypen's funeral, Patty was very low indeed. Doctor and nurses held their breath as their patient hovered on the borderland of the Valley of Shadow, and

[243]

Patty's father, with Nan sobbing in his arms, awaited the dread verdict or the word of glorious hope.

Patty stirred restlessly, her breathing laboured and difficult. " I—did—promise," she said in very low, but clear tones, " but I didn't—oh, I didn't—*want* to—I didn't——" her voice trailed away to silence.

" What *is* that promise? " whispered the doctor to Nan. " It's been troubling her——"

" I don't know at all. She usually tells me her troubles, but I don't know what this means."

There was a slight commotion below stairs. The doctor looked at a nurse, and she moved noiselessly out to command quiet.

Patty's eyes opened wide, they looked very blue, and their glance was more nearly rational than it had been.

" Sh! " she said, weakly. " Listen! It *is!* Yes, it *is*. Tell him to come up, I want to see him."

" Who is it? " asked the doctor. " She mustn't see anybody."

" I must," whimpered Patty, beginning to cry; " it's Little Billee; I want him now."

" For heaven's sake, she's rational! " exclaimed the doctor. " Bring him up, whoever he is, if she says so! No matter if it's an elephant, bring him at once!"

Half frightened, Nan went out into the hall. Sure enough, big Bill Farnsworth was halfway upstairs.

" I heard her!" he said, in a choked voice, " she said she wanted me——"

" Come," said Nan, and led the way.

Softly Farnsworth stepped inside the door, gently as a woman he took Patty's thin little hand in his two big strong ones, as he sat down in a chair beside her bed.

" Little Billee," and Patty smiled faintly, " I want somebody to strong me—I'm so weak— you can——"

"Yes, dear," and firmly holding her hand in one of his, Farnsworth softly touched her eyelids with his fingertips, and the white lids fell over the blue eyes, and with a contented little sigh, Patty sank into a natural sleep, the first in many days.

Released from his nervous tension, the doctor's set features relaxed. He looked in gratified amazement at the sleeping girl, and at the two astonished nurses.

" She will live," he said, softly. " But it is

[245]

like a miracle. On no account let her be awakened; but you may move, sir. She is in a sound sleep of exhaustion."

Farnsworth rose,—laying down Patty's hand lightly as a snowflake,—and soundlessly left the room.

Nan and Mr. Fairfield followed, after a moment.

They found the big fellow looking out of the hall window. At their footsteps, he turned, making no secret of the fact that he was wiping the tears from his eyes.

"I didn't know—" he said, brokenly, "until yesterday. I was in Chicago,—I made the best connections I could, and raced up here. Have I—is she—all right now?"

"Yes," and Fred Fairfield grasped Farnsworth's hand. "Undoubtedly you saved her life. It was the crisis. If she could sleep—they said,—and she is sleeping."

"Thank God!" and the honest blue eyes of the big Westerner filled again with tears.

"Thank *you*, too," cried Nan, and she shook his hand with fervour. "Come into my sitting-room, and tell me all about it. How did Patty know you were here?"

"Didn't you tell her?" Bill looked amazed.

The Crisis

"No; she must have heard your voice—downstairs——"

"But I scarcely spoke above my breath!"

"She heard it,—or divined your presence somehow, for she said you were there and she wanted you,—the first rational words she has spoken!"

"Bless her heart! Perhaps she heard me, perhaps it was telepathy. I don't know, or care. She wanted me, and I was there. I am glad."

The big man looked so proud and yet so humble as he said this, that Nan forgot her dislike and distrust of him, and begged him to stay with them.

"Oh, no," he said. "That wouldn't do. I'll be in New York a few weeks now, at the Excelsior. I'll see you often,—and Patty when I may,—but I won't stay here, thanks. I'm so happy to have been of service, and always command me, of course."

Farnsworth bowed and went off, and the two Fairfields looked at each other.

"What an episode!" exclaimed Nan. "Did he really save her life, Fred?"

"He probably did. We can never say for

certain, but at that crisis, a natural sleep is a Godsend. He induced it, whether by a kind of mesmerism, or whether because Patty cares so much for him, I can't say. I hate to think the latter——"

"Why?"

"Well, for one thing, you know that story Van Reypen tells, about Farnsworth trying to get Patty to go on the operatic stage——"

"I never was sure about that—we didn't hear it so very straight."

"Well, and Farnsworth is not altogether of—of our own sort——"

"You mean, not the aristocrat Phil is?"

"Something like that."

"Well, all that doesn't matter just now. If the doctor says Bill saved Patty's life, I shall always adore him, and I shall erect a very high monument to his honour. So there, now!"

Nan was almost gay. The revulsion of feeling brought about by Patty's improved condition made her so joyous she had to express it in some way.

First, she tiptoed to the door, and beckoned the nurse out. From her she demanded and received assurance that Patty was really past

[248]

the present danger, and barring relapse or complication, would get well.

Then she flew to the telephone and told Mona, leaving her to pass the glad news on to the others.

She wanted to call up Van Reypen, but was uncertain whether to do so or not. He was but just returned from his aunt's burial, and the time seemed inopportune. Yet, he would be so anxious to hear, and perhaps no one else would tell him.

So she called him, telling the servant who answered, who she was, and saying Mr. Van Reypen might speak to her or not, as he wished.

" Of course I want to speak to you," Phil's deep voice responded; " how is she? "

" Better, really better. She will get well, if there are no setbacks."

"Oh, *I am* so glad. Mrs. Nan, I have been so saddened these last few days. I couldn't go to you as I wished, because of affairs here. Now, dear old aunty is laid to rest, and soon I must come over. I don't hope to see Patty, but I want a talk with you. May I come to-night? "

" Surely, Philip. Come when you will, you are always welcome."

[249]

"But I don't know," Nan said to Fred Fairfield, "what Philip will say when he knows who it was that brought about Patty's recovery."

"Need he know? Need anybody know? Perhaps when Patty can have a say in the matter, she will not wish it known. The nurses won't tell. Need we?"

"Perhaps not," said Nan, thoughtfully.

CHAPTER XVIII

PATTY'S FORTUNE

THOUGH Patty's recovery was steady, it was very, very slow. The utmost care was taken against relapse; and so greatly had the disease sapped her strength, that it seemed well-nigh impossible for her to regain it. But skilled nursing proved effectual in the end, and the day came at last when Patty was allowed to see one or two visitors.

Adele was the first to be admitted to the presence of the convalescent. She had come down from Fern Falls as soon as the welcome word reached her that she might see Patty. She was to remain with her but a few moments, and then, if no harm resulted, the next day Mona was to be admitted.

Patty herself was eager to see her friends, and showed decided interest in getting arrayed for the occasion of Adele's visit. This greatly pleased Nurse Adams for until now, Patty had turned a deaf ear to all news or discussion of the outer world, and had shown a listless

[251]

apathy when Nan or her father told her of the doings of the young people of her set. This had been partly due to her weakened condition and partly to her brooding in secret over the promise she had given Mrs. Van Reypen. She had never mentioned this subject to Nan, nor had they yet told Patty of Mrs. Van Reypen's death. The doctor forbade the introduction of any exciting topic, and this news of her dear old friend would surely startle her.

"I'll wear my blue *crêpe de chine* negligée," Patty directed; "the one with lace insets. And the cap with Empire bows and rosebuds."

"Delightful!" said Miss Adams. "It will be a pleasant change to see you dressed up for company."

"I haven't been dolled up in so long, I 'most forget how to primp, but I daresay it will come back to me, for I'm a very vain person."

"That's good," and Nurse Adams laughed. "It's always a good sign when a patient revives an interest in clothes."

"I doubt if I ever lost mine, really. It was probably lying dormant all through the late unpleasantness. Now, please, my blue brocade mules and some blue stockings,—or, no,—white ones, I think."

[252]

Miss Adams brushed the mop of golden curls, that had been so in the way during the severe illness, and massed them high on the little head, crowning all with the dainty cap of lace and ribbons.

"Now, I will gracefully recline on my boudoir couch, and await the raising of the curtain."

"You darling thing!" cried Adele, as she entered, "if you aren't the same old Patty!"

"'Course I am! Who did you think I would be? Oh, but it's good to see you! I haven't seen a soul but the Regular Army for weeks and months and years!"

Patty had never referred to Farnsworth's presence, and no one had spoken of it to her. They had concluded that she was really unconscious of it, or it had lapsed from her memory.

"And you're looking so well. Your cheeks are quite pink, and, why, I do declare, you look almost pretty!"

"*I* think I look ravishingly beautiful. I've consulted a mirror today for the first time, and I was so glad to see myself again, it was quite like meeting an old friend. How's Jim?"

"Fine. Sent you so many loving messages, I decline to repeat them."

"Dear old Jim. Give him my best. Tomorrow I'm to see Mona. Isn't that gay?"

"Yes, but I'd rather you'd be more interested in my call than to be looking forward to hers."

"You old goose! Do you s'pose I'd had you first, if I didn't love you most?"

"Now, I know you're getting well. You've not lost your knack of making pretty speeches."

"It's a comfort to have somebody to make them to. The doctors were most unimpressionable, and I can't bamboozle Miss Adams with flattery. She won't stand for it!"

The white-garbed nurse smiled at her pretty patient.

"And," Patty went on, "after Mona, I'm to see Elise and the other girls, and then if you please, I'm to be allowed to see some of my boy friends!"

"Oh, you coquette! You're just looking forward with all your eyes to having Chick and Kit and all the rest come in and tell you how well you're looking."

"Yes," and Patty folded her hands demurely. "It's such pleasant hearing, after weeks of looking like a holler-eyed mummy, all skin and bone."

"Patty, you're incorrigible," and Adele laughed fondly at the girl she loved so well. "But you're certainly looking the part of interesting invalid, all right. Isn't she, Mrs. Fairfield?"

"Rather!" said Nan, who had just appeared in the doorway. "And your visit is doing her a lot of good. Why, she looks quite her old self."

"A sort of reincarnated version of her old self, all made over new. By the way, Patty, I saw Maude Kent yesterday."

"Did you, Adele? What is she doing now?"

"Concerts as usual. I heard about her session with your father!" and Adele laughed. "The idea of her thinking you'd dream of the stage!"

"But think what a great tragedienne is lost to the world!" said Patty. "I know I have marvelous talent, but my stern parents refused to let me prove it."

"The most outrageous idea!" declared Nan. "Nobody but that Mr. Farnsworth would have suggested such a thing! I suppose Westerners have a different code of conventions from ours."

"Bill Farnsworth suggest it!" cried Patty.

"Why, Nan, you're crazy! He's the one who kept me from it. Wasn't he, Adele?"

"Why, yes, Mrs. Nan. It was he who went over to Poland Spring with Patty——"

"Yes, that's what I heard. Took Patty over there to see this Kent person about the matter."

"Goodness, gracious me!" Patty exclaimed; "wherever did you get such a mixup, Nansome? Why, it was Little Billee who gave Maude whatfor, because she mentioned the idea! He told her never to dream of it, and made me go straight home."

Nan looked puzzled. "Why," she said, "Philip Van Reypen told me that Mr. Farnsworth put you up to it, and said you were good-looking enough——"

Patty laughed outright. "Oh, Nannie, I remember that! *I* said I was good-looking enough, and Bill said yes, I was *that*,—of course, he had to agree!—but he said that had nothing to do with the matter. And as to Phil, he knew nothing about it. He wasn't there."

"No. Somebody told him, that day he met you all in Boston."

"Oh, fiddle-de-dee! Somebody said that somebody else heard that somebody—Now,

[256]

listen here, Nan, nobody put me up to that stage business 'ceptin' my own little self, and, of course, Maude, who told me about it. But she did nothing wrong in giving me the chance. And it's all past history, only don't you say Little Billee egged me on, because he most emphatically egged me off. Didn't he, Adele?"

"Yes, he did. You told me all about it at the time. Bill Farnsworth was most indignant at Miss Kent, but she was a friend of Chick Channing's and so Bill wouldn't say anything against her."

"There isn't anything against her," declared Patty, "and Little Billee wouldn't say it if there were. But you just remember that he was on the other side of the fence. If anybody sort of approved of it, it was Chick. He thought it would be rather fun, but he didn't take it seriously at all. So you just cross off that black mark you have against Big Bill!"

"I will," promised Nan, and Adele said, "Where is Bill now? Have you seen him of late?"

"No," said Patty; "not since before I was ill. I don't know where he is."

Nan looked at her closely, but it was evident she was speaking in earnest. As they thought, then, she had forgotten the incident of his appearance at her bedside. Perhaps she never really knew of it, as she was so nearly unconscious at the time.

"He is in New York," said Nan, covertly watching Patty.

"Is he?" said Patty, with some animation. "After I get well enough to see men-people, I'd like to have him call."

"Very well," returned Nan, "but now I'm going to take Adele away. The nurse has been making signals to me for five minutes past. You mustn't get overtired with your first visitor, or you can't have others."

But visitors seemed to agree with Patty. Once back in the atmosphere of gay chatter and laughter with her friends, she grew better rapidly, and the roses came back to her cheeks and the strength to her body.

And so, when they thought she could bear it, they told her of Mrs. Van Reypen's death.

"I suspected it," said Patty, her eyes filling with tears, "just because you didn't say anything about her, and evaded my questions. When was it?"

They told her all about it, and then Mr. Fairfield said, "And, my child, in her will was a large bequest for you."

"I know," said Patty, and her fingers locked nervously together. "A hundred thousand million dollars! Or it might as well be. I don't want the money, Daddy."

"But it is yours, and in your trust. You can't well refuse it. Half is for——"

"Yes, I know,—for a Children's Home. But I can't build a house now."

"Don't think about those things until you are stronger. The Home project will keep,—for years, if need be. And when the time comes, all the burdensome details will be in the hands of a Board of Trustees and you needn't carry it on your poor little shoulders."

"It isn't that that's bothering me, but my own half. You don't know *why* she gave me that."

"Why did she?" said Nan, quickly, her woman's mind half divining the truth.

"She made me promise, the last time I saw her, that—that I would marry Philip. And when I said I wouldn't promise, she was very angry, and said then she wouldn't leave me the money. And I was madder than she was, and said I didn't want her old money, and neither I don't, with Philip or without him."

"But what an extraordinary proceeding!" exclaimed Mr. Fairfield. "She tried to buy you!"

"Oh, well, of course she didn't put it that way, but she was all honey and peaches and leaving me fortunes and building Children's Homes until I refused to promise, *then* she turned and railed at me."

"And then——" prompted Nan.

"Then I was mad and I tried to start for home. Then she calmed down and was sweet again, and said she didn't mean to balance the money against the promise, but, well—she kept at me until she *made* me give in."

"And you promised?"

"Yes."

"You poor little Patty," cried Nan; "you poor, dear, little thing! How could she torture you so?"

"It was, Nan," cried Patty, eagerly; "it was just that,—torture. Oh, I'm so glad you can see it! I didn't know *what* to do. She said I mustn't refuse the request of a dying woman, and she grabbed my arm and shook me, and she looked like a—oh, she just looked *terrifying,* you know, and she—well, I guess she hypnotised me into promising."

"Of course she did! It's a perfect shame!" and Nan gathered Patty into her arms.

"It *is* a shame," agreed Mr. Fairfield, smiling at his daughter, "but it won't be such an awfully hard promise to keep, will it, Little Girl? Of course you hated to have it put to you in that manner, but there are less desirable men in this world than Philip Van Reypen."

"I don't want to talk about it," said Patty, and she burst into tears on Nan's shoulder.

"And you sha'n't," returned Nan, caressing her. "Go away, Fred. A man doesn't know how to deal with a case like this. Patty isn't strong enough yet to think of bothersome things. You go away and we'll tell you later what we decide."

Mr. Fairfield rose, grumbling, laughingly, that it was the first time he had ever been called down by his own family. But he went away, saying over his shoulder, "You girls just want to have a tearfest, that's all."

"Tell me all about it, dear," said Nan, as Patty smiled through her tears.

"That's about all, Nancy. But it was such a horrid situation. I do like Phil, but I don't want to make any such promise as that. Of course, Phil has asked me himself, several times, but I've never said yes——"

" Or no?"

" Or no. I don't have to till I get ready, do I? And I surely don't have to give my promise to the aunt of the person most interested. Oh, I'm so sorry she died. I wanted to ask her to let me off. I dreamed about it all the time I was sick. It was like a continual nightmare. Has Phil been here?"

" Yes, two or three times. He wants to see you as soon as you say so."

" How can I see him? Do you suppose he knows of my promise?"

" Very likely she told him. I don't know. But, Patty, don't blame her too much. You know, she was very fond of you, and she worshipped him. It was the wish of her heart,— but, no, she *hadn't* any right to force your promise!"

" That's what she did, she forced it. Nan, am I bound by it?"

" Why, no; that is, not unless you want to be. Or unless——"

" Unless I consider a promise made to a dying person sacred. Well, I'm afraid I do. I've thought over this thing, day in and day out,

[262]

and it seems to me I'd be *wicked* to break a promise given to one who is gone."

"Maybe Philip will let you off."

"No, he won't. I know Phil wants me to marry him, *awfully*, and he'd take me on any terms. This sounds conceited, but I *know*, 'cause he's told me so."

"Well, Patty, why not?"

"That's just it. I don't know why not. Sometimes I think it's just because I don't want to be made to do a thing, whether I choose or not. And then sometimes,——"

"Well?"

"Sometimes I think I don't love Phil enough to marry him. He's a dear, and he's awfully kind and generous and good. And he adores me,—but I don't feel—say, Nan, were you *terribly* in love with father when you married him?"

"I was, Patty. And I still am."

"Yes, I know you are now. But were you before the wedding day?"

"Yes."

"Well, I'm not *terribly* in love with Phil. But he says that will come after we're married. Will it, Nan?"

"It's hard to advise you, Patty. I daren't

say the greater love will come to you,—for I don't know. But don't marry him unless you are sure he is the only man in the world you can love."

" I've got to marry him," said Patty, simply; " I promised."

CHAPTER XIX

A DISTURBING LETTER

THEN the days came when Patty could see anybody and everybody who called upon her. When she could be downstairs in the library or the big cheery living-room, and, as she expressed it, be " folks " once more.

Still flowers were sent to her, still candies and fruit and dainty delicacies arrived in boxes and baskets, and friends sent books, pictures, and letters. Her mail was voluminous, so much so that Nurse Adams who still tarried, was pressed into service as amanuensis and general secretary.

The men had begun to be allowed to call, and Patty saw Cameron and Channing, who happened to call first.

" My, but it's good to gaze on your haughty beauty again! " said Chick; " I've missed you more than tongue can tell! "

" Me too," said Kit. " I wanted to telephone,

but they wouldn't let me. Said I was too near and dear to be heard without being seen,—like the children, or whoever it is."

"I wish you had," and Patty laughed. "I was longing to babble over a telephone, as we used to do, Kit."

"Yes, in the early days of our courtship, when we were twenty-one!"

"Speak for yourself, John! I'll leave it to Chick,—*do* I look twenty-one!"

"I should say not! You look sweet sixteen, or thereabouts."

He was right, for Patty did look adorably young and sweet. She had on a Frenchy tea-gown of pale green silk, bubbling over with tulle frills of the same shade, touched here and there with tiny rosebuds. A fetching cap of matching materials, was, Nan declared, a mere piece of affectation, but it accented her invalidism, and was vastly becoming. Her face, still pale from her illness, was of a waxen hue, but a warm pink had begun to glow in her cheeks and her blue eyes were as twinkling and roguish as ever.

"And what's more," Patty went on, "I won't be twenty-one till next May,—and that's ages away yet."

[266]

A Disturbing Letter

"Yes, about half a year!" retorted Kit, "so I'm not so very far out, my little old lady! Did you get all the tokens I sent you?"

"Guess I did. I'm acknowledging 'em up as fast as I can. I had such oodles of stuff. I begrudge the flowers that came while I was too lost to the world to see them, but enough have come since to make up. You'll get your receipts in due time."

"Thanks. I was afraid mine were lost in the shuffle. I say, Patty, when can you go out for a spin?"

"Not this week. Next, maybe."

"Go with me first?"

"No, me," put in Chick. "I've a limousine, he has only a runabout."

"Lots more fun in a runabout. Besides, I asked you first."

"What fun!" cried Patty, clapping her hands. "It's like a dance. I'm going to have a programme. Wait, here's one."

Patty found an old dance programme in the desk near her, and Kit kindly essayed to rub off the names. Then with his fountain pen he wrote over the dances, "Limousine Ride." "Runabout Spin." "Walk." "Skate." "Opera." "Dance." "Matinée," and a host of other pleasures to which Patty might reasonably expect to be invited soon.

But she would only allow them one each, and after they had written their names after the motor-car rides, they were shooed away by ever watchful Nan, who would not allow Patty to become overtired.

Then, one morning, in the mail came a communication from Mrs. Van Reypen's lawyer. It informed Patty of the legacy left her. As Mrs. Van Reypen had said, there was a bequest of fifty thousand dollars to Patty herself, and another fifty thousand in trust for a fund for a Children's Home. The details of the institution were left entirely to Patty's discretion, and she was instructed, if in need of more funds, to apply to Philip Van Reypen.

Also was enclosed a note which Mrs. Van Reypen had written and directed to be given to Patty after her death.

"I'm afraid to open it, Nan," said Patty, trembling as she looked at the sealed epistle.

"I don't wonder you feel so, dear. Let me read it first."

Gladly Patty passed it over, for she had no secrets from Nan, and her nerves were not yet as strong as before her illness.

A Disturbing Letter

Nan read it, and then said. "You need have no fear, Patty, it's a dear note. Listen:

"My Dear Little Patty:

"I am afraid I made you sorrowful when I talked to you and urged you to promise the thing I asked of you. But don't feel hard toward me. I have your interests at heart as well as Philip's, and I know that what you have promised will mean your life's happiness. Now, about the Children's Home. If you feel that after all it is too great a tax on your time or strength to take it in charge, don't do so. Turn it all over to some one else. You and Philip can decide on the right person for the work. But I trust you will have an interest in it, and see to it that the furnishings and little comforts are as you and I would choose were we working together. This note, dear, is to say good-bye. I shall not see you again, but I die content, knowing you will love and look after my boy. It seemed strange at first to your girl heart, but you will come to love him as your own, and your life together will be filled with joy and peace. Good-bye, my child, have a kindly remembrance in your heart for your old friend,

"LADY VAN."

Patty was crying as Nan finished. It so brought back the fine but eccentric old lady, and so renewed that dreadful promise, that the girl was completely upset.

"You see," she sobbed, "I've got to marry him. This is like a voice from the grave, holding me to my vow. Isn't it, Nan?"

"Patty, look here. Do you want to marry Phil, or don't you?"

At the quick, sharp question, Patty looked up with a start.

"Honest, Nan, I don't know."

"Then you ought to find out. It's this way, Patty. If you do want to marry him, or if you are willing to, there's no use in fussing over this promise business. If you don't, and if you are sure you don't, then you must break that promise. But, you've got to be sure first."

"How can I be sure?"

"Is there anybody else you care for?"

"N—no."

"Kit Cameron is very much in love with you, Patty. He asked me when you were ill, if I thought he had a chance. Has he?"

"Not the ghost of a chance! Kit's an old dear, and I like him a heap, but he's a worse flirt than I am. Mercy, Nan, I wouldn't marry him for a minute!"

"Chick Channing?"

"No. He's a lovely boy to play around with, but not to take for a life partner. Oh, well, I s'pose it'll have to be Phil, after all."

"Your father and I would like that."

"And Mrs. Van Reypen seemed to think she'd like it; and I feel quite sure Phil would like it; and it doesn't matter about little old me!"

"Patty! stop talking like that! You know nobody wants you to do a thing you don't want to do! And don't get mad at your Nan, who has only your best interests at heart!"

"'Deed I won't! I'm a brute! A big, ugly, horrid brute! Nansome, you're my good angel. Now, let's drop this subject for a time,—or I'll get so nervous I'll fly to the moon!"

"Of course you will! And you're not going to be bothered out of your life, either. You put it all out of your mind, and come with me, out for a ridy-by. Then back and have a nice little nap. Then a 'normous big luncheon; and then dress yourself all up pretty for callers."

"What an entrancing programme! Nan, sometimes I think you're a genius! I sure do!"

The enticing programme was carried out, and

[271]

that afternoon Van Reypen came to call. It was the first time he had seen Patty since her illness, and she rather dreaded the meeting.

But Philip was so cheery and kindly that Patty felt at ease at once.

"Dear little girl," he said, taking both her hands, "how good to see you looking so well. I've been *so* anxious about you."

"Needn't be any more," said Patty, smiling up at him. "I'm all well now, and never going to be sick again. But I've been feeling very sorry for you, Phil."

"Thank you, dear. It *is* hard, the old house seems so empty and lonely. But Aunty Van rather wanted to go, and she bade me think of her only with pleasant memories, and not with mourning."

"She was always thoughtful of others' feelings. And, Phil, how she did love you."

"She did. And you, too; why, I never supposed she could care for any one outside our family as she cared for you."

"She was awfully kind to me."

"And you were to her. You were mighty good, Patty, to put up with her queer little notions the way you always did. And I say, do you know what she told me just before she

[272]

died? She told me that you said you would learn to love me. Oh, Patty, did you? I don't doubt her word, but sometimes she thought a thing was so, when really it was only her strong wish. So I *must* ask you. I didn't mean to ask you today,—I meant to wait till you are strong and well again. But, darling, you look so sweet and dear, and I haven't seen you for so long, I can't wait. Tell me, Patty, *did* you tell Aunty Van that?"

Patty hesitated. A yes or no here meant so much,—and yet she couldn't put him off.

"Tell me," he urged; "you must have said something of the sort. Even if she exaggerated, she wouldn't make it *all* up. What did you tell her, dear?"

The two were alone in the library. The dusk was just beginning,—the lights not yet turned on. Patty, in a great easy chair, sat near the wood fire, which had burned down to a few glowing embers. Van Reypen, restless, had been stalking about the room. Now, he came near to her, and pushing up an ottoman, he sat down by her.

"You must tell me," he said, in a low, tense voice. "I can't bear it if you don't. I won't

[273]

ask you anything more,—I'll go right away, if you say so,—but, Patty, dearest, tell me if you told Aunty Van that you would learn to love me."

Phil's dark, handsome face looked into her own. With a feeling as of a tightening round her heart, Patty realised that his eyes were very like his aunt's, that their impelling gaze would yet make her say yes. And, fascinated, she gazed back, until, coerced, she breathed a low "yes."

Then, appalled at the look that came to his face she covered her eyes with her hands, whispering, "Go away, Phil. You said you'd go away if I wanted you to, and I do want you to. Please go."

Van Reypen leaned nearer. "I will go, Little Sweetheart. I can bear to go now. You have made me so happy with that one little word. The rest can wait. Good-bye, you will call me back soon, I know."

Bending down he dropped a light kiss on the curly golden hair, and went away, happy in the knowledge of Patty's love, and almost amused at what he thought was her shyness in acknowledging it.

When she heard the street door close, Patty

looked up. Her face was white, and she was nervously trembling.

"Nan," she called; "Nan!"

Nan came in from another room. "What is it, Patty, dear? Where is Philip?"

"He's gone. Oh, Nan, I kept my promise."

"You did! What do you mean? Are you engaged to Philip? Then why did he go?"

Patty laughed, but it was a little hysterical. "I sent him away. No, we're not engaged, that is, I don't think we are. But I suppose we will be."

"Patty, behave yourself. Brace up, now, and tell me what you're talking about. Any one would think getting engaged was a funeral or some such occasion!"

Patty shook herself, and smiled at Nan.

"I am a goose, I suppose. I don't know whether I'm glad or sorry, but I told Phil I'd learn to love him."

"H'm, I don't see as you've bound yourself to anything very desperate! You can doubtless learn, if you study hard enough."

"Don't tease me, Nan. I'm not sure I want to learn."

"Then don't! Patty, sometimes you're perfectly ridiculous!"

[275]

"Huh! Just 'cause *you* happened to get a perfectly splendid man like my father, and didn't have to think twice, you think *everybody* can decide in a hurry!"

Nan burst into laughter. "Oh, you are *too* funny!" she cried, and Patty had to laugh, too.

"I suppose I am," she said, dolefully, "to you. But to me it doesn't seem funny a bit."

"Forgive me, dear," said Nan, repentantly; "I won't laugh any more. Tell me about it."

"It's that old promise thing. Mrs. Van told Phil I had told her I would learn to love him, and he asked me if I did. And I had to say yes. And of course I couldn't tell him she *made* me promise. Now, could I?"

"I don't know. It *is* a little serious, Patty, unless, as I said before, unless you want to learn to love him. Do you?"

"I don't know, but I don't think so. I wish to goodness he wouldn't bother me about it!"

"He sha'n't! Patty, it is a shame for you to be bothered if you don't want to be. Now, I'll help you out. I'll tell Phil, myself, that you're not well enough yet to be troubled about serious matters, and he must wait till you are. He won't be angry, I can explain it to him."

"I don't care whether he's angry or not. It

isn't that, Nan. It's that just the little bit I said to him, he takes to mean—everything."

"Of course he does, Patty. You can't tell a man you'll learn to love him unless you mean that you expect to succeed and that you'll marry him. What else *could* you mean?"

"Of course, if I said it of my own accord. But, don't you see, Nan, that I only said it because I promised her I would, and it doesn't seem fair, that I should have to say it because she made me."

"You're right, Patty, it *doesn't*. And you ought not to be held by that infamous performance! I just begin to see it as it is, and I am not going to have you tortured. You don't really love Phil, or you'd know it; and this 'promise' and 'learning to love him' is all foolishness. I'm going to tell him, or have Fred do so, of that promise business, and then if he wants to ask you again, and let you answer of your own will, and not by anybody's coercion, very well."

"Oh, Nan, what a duck you are! What would I ever do without you! Will you really do that? I tried to tell Phil how it was, but he was so—so——"

"Precipitate?"

"Yes, that; but I meant more that he was so glad to have me say that *yes,* that it seemed too bad to tell him that awful story about his aunt."

"It *is* an awful story, but he ought to know it. Why, he'd rather know it. You two couldn't live all your lives with that secret between you—could you?"

"Of course we couldn't."

"And then, too, it isn't fair to him. If you're answering his question under duress,—I never did know what duress meant,—but anyway, if you're answering his questions at his aunt's commands, he certainly ought to know it. It's wrong to let him think it's your own answer, if it isn't."

"That's so," and Patty looked greatly relieved. "Say, Nan, when can you tell him?"

"Oh, I can't do it. I'll get your father to. He's the proper one, anyway."

"Yes, I guess he is," sighed Patty. "Oh, what do poor little girls do who haven't such kind parents? And now I wonder if it isn't time for my beef tea!"

CHAPTER XX

BETTER THAN ANYBODY ELSE

IT was the next afternoon that Farnsworth called. He had not seen Patty since the day she was so very ill, but he had telephoned or called every day to inquire after her. Today he was allowed to see her, and as he entered the library, his face was radiant with sunny smiles.

Patty looked up, smiling too, and held out her hands in greeting. From the lace cap that crowned her hair, to the tips of her dainty slippers, she was all in white, and her pale face and waxen hands made her look so like an angel that big, strapping Bill held his breath as he looked at her.

"Are you really there?" he asked; "are you fastened to earth? I somehow feel afraid you'll waft off into the ether, you look so ethereal."

"No, indeed! I'm here to stay. I've a pretty strong liking for this old world and I've no desire to flee away just yet."

"Good! It's great to see you again," and Farnsworth took a seat beside her. "I'm thinking you'll be getting out of doors soon."

"I hope so. But I'm having a beautiful time convalescing. Everybody is so good to me, and I'm showered with presents, as if I were—engaged!"

"And I hear that you are." Bill looked at her steadily. "I'm told that you're betrothed to Van Reypen, and I want to be among the first to wish you all the joy there is in the world."

"Who told you?" and Patty looked startled.

"A little bird," Farnsworth smiled at her gently. "I am very glad for you, dear. Philip is a big, strong-hearted chap, and he can give you all you want and deserve."

"'Most anybody could do that," said Patty, a little shortly, for it seemed to her that Farnsworth took the news of her engagement rather easily.

"No. I couldn't. There are not many men like Van Reypen; rich, well-born, intellectual, and kind. Moreover, he has prestige and an acknowledged place in the best society; all of which goes to make up the atmosphere of life that best suits you,—you petted butterfly."

Bill's smile robbed the words of any effect of satire or reproof.

"Am I a feather-headed rattlepate?" and Patty treated the young man to her best and prettiest pout.

"Not entirely. But you like to have all about you in harmony and good taste. Nor are you to blame. You are born to the purple,—and all that that signifies."

"Aren't you?"

"I?" Farnsworth looked amazed. "No, Patty; I am what they call a self-made man. My people are plain people, and my childhood was one of rough experiences,—even hardships."

"All the more credit to you, Little Billee, for turning out a polished gentleman."

"But I'm not, dear. I've picked up enough of social customs not to make awkward mistakes, but I have not the innate breeding of the Van Reypens."

Farnsworth was not looking at Patty, he was staring into vacancy, and looked as if he were talking more to himself than to her.

"Rubbish!" said Patty, gaily, annoyed at herself for feeling the truth of his words. "You're a splendid old Bill, and whoever says

[281]

a word against you is no friend of mine! So be careful, sir, what you say against yourself."

"You're a loyal little friend, Patty, and I'm more glad than you can realise to know that it is so. Now, you're going to do all you can to grow stronger, aren't you? It hurts me to see you so white and wan-looking. I wish I could give you some of my big strength,—I've more than I know what to do with."

At this speech Patty blushed a rosy crimson, and Farnsworth's remark about her wan looks lost its point.

"Why the apple blossoms in your cheeks, Little Girl?" and he smiled at her evident confusion.

"Would you give me of your strength, Bill,— if—if I were—were—dying——"

"Wouldn't I! I'd snatch you back from old Charon, if you had one foot in his boat!"

Patty looked at him, with a queer uncertainty in her eyes. Twice she tried to say something, and couldn't; and then Farnsworth said softly:

"As I did,—although I doubt if you knew it."

"Did you, Billee? *Really?* I thought it was a dream,—wasn't it?"

"You mean—that day——"

"Yes."

"No, Patty, it was not a dream. I chanced to come in, and when I asked about you, you must have heard my voice, for you called out to me——"

"And you came."

"Yes. And you wanted some of my strength, —I gave it to you by putting you to sleep. That was what you needed most."

"Was that the crisis, Bill?"

"They said so, dear. I am glad I could help."

"You saved my life."

"I'm not sure of that, but I wish I had, for you know there is a convention that gives saved lives to the savers."

"Take it, then," said Patty, impulsively.

Farnsworth gave her a long look. "I wouldn't want it because you thought you *ought* to give it to me."

"Yet that is why I'm giving it to Philip."

"He didn't save your life!"

"No, I mean I'm giving it to him because I think I ought to."

"What *do* you mean?"

And then Patty told him the whole story of her promise to Mrs. Van Reypen, and her consequent enforced betrothal to Philip.

Farnsworth's blue eyes opened wide. "And he takes you on those terms!"

"Oh, he doesn't know about the promise. But what else can I do, Little Billee? I can't break a promise made to a dying woman, and—too— I like Phil——"

"Like isn't enough," said Farnsworth, sternly. "Do you love him, Patty?"

"I—I guess so——" she stammered, a little frightened at his vehemence.

And at that very moment Philip Van Reypen appeared.

"Hello, Peaches," he said gaily to Patty. "How do, Farnsworth? And how's our interesting invalid today?"

"I'm fine," returned Patty. "Getting better by the minute. 'Spect to go out coasting soon. Better get your sleds ready, we may have snow any day——"

Patty was babbling on to cover a certain constraint in the attitude of the two men. But almost immediately, Farnsworth took his leave, gently declining Patty's plea to stay longer.

"Let him go," said Philip, as the street door closed behind Bill; "I want to see you alone. See here, Patty, what's this about a promise to Aunty Van?"

Better than Anybody Else

"Who told you?"

"Your father. Sent and asked me to come to his office, so I went, and he told me the whole story. You poor little girl! I'm *so* sorry it happened, and I've come to ask you to forgive Aunty Van. She was all wrong to do such a thing, but honestly, she was actuated by right motives. She loved you so, and she loved me, and she was so sure we were made for each other. I'm sure of that, too,—but if you're not, you're to say so, and not think you're bound by a promise to *anybody*."

"But I did promise her——"

"Forget it! In your dealings with me, you're to deal only with me. There's no go-between or dictator or even adviser; only just our two selves. But before we begin on our affairs, I want this other matter settled for all time. Promise me that you will never again even think of that promise that she wrung from you. You *must*, or I can't have loving memories of Aunty Van. Also, I want you to tell me truly, whether you want to look after the Children's Home scheme or not. If it's a burden, you're not to have anything to do with it. See?"

"How kind you are, Phil. Yes, I do want to help with the Home project, but I don't want

[285]

to be at the head of the Board,—or whatever has charge of it. I want to tend to the furnishings and little comforty things for the kiddies, but can't somebody else build it?"

"Of course they can! You dear Baby, do you think you're to have all that on your poor little shoulders? It shall all be just as you say. And you are to do as much or as little as you like. Of course, you're not even to think of it, till you're all well and strong again. Now, as to your own bequest from Aunty Van. I can't tell you how glad I am she left you a little pin-money——"

"A little pin-money!" exclaimed Patty, raising her eyes heavenward.

"Well, an enormous fortune,—if you like that better. But at any rate, it's yours, to do as you please with. I don't suppose you really need it, but——"

"I don't need it for myself, Phil, but oh, I'm going to do such lovely things with it for my girls! I shall use it for their vacation trips and —that is, part of it. Part of it, I'm going to spend on myself—oh, I have the delightfullest plans!"

"All right, Pattykins, do what you will, as long as it pleases your own dear self. And now, we come to what interests me most. I decline to have you for my very own, if you consent *only* because Aunty Van made you promise to do so. Cut that all out,—and let's begin again. Will you promise me,—*me,* mind you,—not any one else *for* me,—to learn to love me?"

And now Patty was her own roguish self again. The release from the bugbear promise was so great, that she considered gaily what Phil was asking now.

"Well," she began, looking provokingly pretty, "suppose I say I'll *try* to learn to love you——"

"Oh, try—to endeavour—to attempt—to make a stab at it! But, all right, I'll take that crumb of a promise. You'll *try* to learn to love me. Patty, *I'm* going to be the teacher, and if you'll try,—and you'll have to, since you've promised,—by Jove, I'll *make* you learn!"

"Very well," and Patty's eyes danced; "when you going to begin?"

"Right off, this minute. And never stop, short of success?"

Van Reypen looked very handsome, his dark hair tossed back from his broad forehead, his dark eyes alight with love and determination.

He was the sort of man who meets any circumstances with graceful un-selfconscious ease, and he sat back in his chair, looking at Patty with an air of assured proprietorship, that amused rather than irritated her.

"But I'm not engaged to you," and Patty shook her lace-capped head till her curls bobbed.

"No? Oh, *do* be! Let's be *that*, at least."

"What! engaged before I've learned to love you! Nevaire!"

"All right, Sweetness. I'll wait. But it won't be long. The poet babbles of 'love's protracted growing,' but ours won't be so terribly protracted, I promise you! I'll give you a week to decide in,—and that's too long——"

"A week! I couldn't begin to get ready to think about it in that time! Give me a month, and I'll go you."

"All right, your wish is law. A month from today, then, you're to complete your lessons, and graduate a full-fledged ladylove of your humble servant."

"I don't think you're so awfully humble, Philip."

"Can't be, while I have you to be proud of!

Oh, Patty, do decide quicker'n a month! That seems a century! Say a fortnight."

"Nope. A month it is, before I need to say yes or no to your question. One more month of gay girlish freedom. Oh, Phil, I couldn't be tied down to any one man! I want to flirt with all of them!"

"Do it in this month, then. For I warn you, after thirty-one more days, your flirtations must be laid aside, with your wax doll and Britannia teaset."

"You seem pretty positive!"

"Faint heart never won fair lady. I've lots of faults, but a faint heart isn't one of them. You're the girl for me, but you don't quite know it for sure,—*yet*. So I'm going to show you the truth, and gently but firmly lead you to it!"

Philip kept the conversation in this light key, and when he went away, Patty retained the impression of a very charming afternoon with him.

"He *is* nice," she said to Nan, after telling her all about it; "You feel so sort of sure of him all the time. He always does the right thing."

"Yes," said Nan.

Next day brought many visitors, but among

the most welcome was Baby Milly, or Middy, as she called herself, and as Patty always called her.

"Such a booful Patty!" the child exclaimed, delighted at seeing her again after so long a time. "Middy loves you dreful! See, Middy b'inged lot o' Naws!"

"She means Noahs, ma'am," explained the nurse who had Milly in charge. "They're the dolls from her Noah's Ark."

Sure enough, the baby had the four straight-garmented puppets that represent in painted wood, the patriarch and his three sons.

They were up in Patty's boudoir and the little one gaily stood her cherished toys round among the small ferns in the window-box.

Suddenly Patty grabbed her up and carried her off to have a feast of bread and jam and milk.

"Nice party," the guest remarked. "Des Patty an' Middy. Ve'y nice party."

After the party, the little one was taken home, and so it was not until she went to her room that night, that Patty discovered the four "Naws" still marching through her ferns.

"Blessed baby!" she said to herself, as she

collected the illustrious quartette, and laid them on the table to be returned to their owner the next day.

Then Patty threw herself in a big chair, to think over her problems. She hadn't told Farnsworth that she was not now engaged to Philip, and she didn't quite like to tell him, though why, she couldn't say.

"I wonder who I like best of anybody in all the world," she mused, as she played idly with Middy's toys. "I'm as uncertain of that, as I am which of these four statuettes I prefer."

She looked critically at the Noah, and at Shem, Ham and Japheth; a little undecided as to which was which, so similar were they in every respect save as to the colours of their long one-piece gowns.

She stood them in a row on the table. "That's Philip," looking at one of them; "that's Little Billee; that's Kit, and the yellow one is Chick Channing. I've come to like Chick a lot,—more'n Kit, I believe. Now, let's see. S'pose I had to lose one of these four forever; which could I best spare."

The game grew exciting. Patty, sitting on one foot, leaned toward the table, middle finger-tip caught against her thumb, ready to snap the least desirable into limbo.

"Sorry," she said, "but old Kit must go." She snapped her fingers, and luckless Kit flew across the room.

Patty's face fell. "It's a hard world! But I'm going to fight this thing to a finish. And there's no use mincing matters, if another had to go—it would, of course, be Chick."

Another flick of her slender fingers, and Channing flew up in the air and landed on the high mantel.

"Now then," and Patty knew that a momentous decision lay before her. There remained Philip and Bill Farnsworth.

Patty clasped her hands, rested her chin upon them and stared at the brown and red-coated gentlemen still standing before her.

"Phil is such a dear," she reasoned, as if trying to convince herself; "and he certainly does worship the ground I walk on. But there's something about Bill—dear Little Billee! I wonder what it is about him—And he *did* save my life—I think I like him for his strength. I never saw anybody so strong—he always makes me think of Sir Galahad;—'His strength was as the strength of ten because his heart was

Better than Anybody Else

pure.' Little Billee's heart is pure,—pure gold. I—somehow, I know it by a sort of intuition. And yet, Phil—oh, Philip is a gentleman, of course, I know that, but Bill is nature's nobleman—well any way, just at this minute, I like Little Billee better than anybody in the world! So, there now!"

With a well-aimed flick of her fingertips, Patty set Philip spinning, and it was a week later that she found him in her work-basket.

She had the grace to look a little ashamed of herself, but the fire of determination was in her eye, and a rosy flush tinted her cheeks.

Then a mischievous smile came to the corners of her mouth, and on an impulse she caught up the telephone from the stand, and called the Excelsior Hotel.

In a few moments Farnsworth's " Hello " sounded in her ear.

" It's Patty," she said, in a small, timid voice.

" Well, I'm glad. Are we to have a little chat? "

" No,—I just wanted to tell you—to tell you——"

" Yes; dear Little Girl,—what is it? "

" I can't seem to tell you after all."

" Shall I come over there? "

[293]

"Oh, no, it's too late. I only wanted to say that—that I'm not really engaged to anybody—now."

"Thank heaven! and,—do you want to be?"

"Oh, no! Not for a month. I've got that long to make up my mind in."

"Good! May I see you in the meantime?"

"Not unless you take that laugh out of your voice! I do believe you're making fun of me."

"I can't help a laugh in my voice when the dull world has suddenly turned to rosy sunlight! Tell me, Apple Blossom, is that all you called up to say?"

"No," and Patty's eyes grew luminous; "I *was* going to say something else——"

"What was it,—tell me,—Patty-sweet,——"

"Only—that at this present moment,—just for *one little minute*, you know, I like—you—better—than—anybody else in all the world!"

And with a sudden click, Patty hung up the receiver, and buried her burning face in her hands.

THE END

[294]